Misery Range

Bay of
Bountiful

Eden Glade

Mt
Molar

Twisty River

Cascade Canyon

Grandad's
Gully

Puzzling
Plains

Col

Cliffs
of
Calamity

Mt
Monstrous

Mother's
Knee Hill

Ridge of Rising
Flame

Swamp of
Children's Wishes

Tree of Wailing
Witches

Meadow of
Dreams

Ancient
Forest

Mystic

Home

Lunch
Pass

The
ISLAND

Home
Lagoon

Granny's Pass

Paradise Peninsula

For Phil

-JR

Published by Dragon Brothers Books Ltd
www.dragonbrothersbooks.com
Text © 2017 James Russell. Illustrations © 2017 Dragon Brothers Books.
A catalogue record for this book is available from the National Library of New Zealand. The moral rights of the author have been asserted. This book is copyright. Except for the purposes of fair reviewing no part of this publication may be reproduced or transmitted in any form or by any means, electronic or mechanical, including photocopying or recording, or stored in any information storage and retrieval system, without permission in writing from the publisher.
ISBN: 978-0-473-37621-5
Digital animations created by www.blacktortoise.co.nz
Cover illustration: Kerem Beyit
Internal vignettes: Suleyman Temiz
Chapter icon: istock

THE DRAGON DEFENDERS

BOOK ONE

"So gripping…"
Finn Buckley, age 11

"The bomb!"
Seamus O'Sullivan, age 11

"Awesome!"
Ari O'Malley, age 10

"Exciting from the very start!"
Theo Head, age 11

"As good as Harry Potter…"
Pippa Montgomerie, age 9

A Dragon Brothers Book by

JAMES RUSSELL

www.dragonbrothersbooks.com

Sign up to find out when the next chapter book in the series comes out.

Simply visit **www.dragonbrothersbooks.com** and enter your email address. We'll keep you updated on new books, and we'll send you an email whenever anything cool happens!

Books in the series

Or, for younger readers

The Dragon Brothers Trilogy

The Dragon Defenders series grew out of The Dragon Brothers Trilogy – children's picture books for children aged 3-7.

How to use this book

This book is unlike any other you've seen. Of course, it works just like a normal book; you start reading at the start, and read right through to the end. That will work just fine.

But you can also enjoy it another way. You can download the free 'AR Reads' app onto a smartphone or tablet, point it at parts of the book and watch it become reality.

Your choice!

Here's how:

Step 1. Download the free 'AR Reads' app*.
You'll find this on the App Store, or on Google Play.

Step 2. Start up the app.

Step 3. Follow the set-up instructions.

Step 4. Point your device's camera at the pictures on the pages marked with a phone/tablet at the bottom.

*If you already have the AR Reads app downloaded onto your device, you'll need to check for updates in order for the app to work on The Dragon Defenders. To use this app, your device will need to have an internet connection.

CHAPTER 1

"Coco – flush them out!"

Two fat pheasants had disappeared into the bushes thirty yards away at the edge of the clearing, and Flynn intended to have at least one of them for dinner. He whistled softly to Coco, a slowly rising tone – the command for the dog to circle around to the left and approach their prey from the side. She responded immediately, padding softly away from the brothers. Flynn raised his slingshot and drew it back to his cheek, taking careful aim.

"Are you sure you don't need me to take the shot?" Paddy whispered in his ear. "You might miss."

Flynn didn't reply, but couldn't help but smile. His little brother could always be relied upon for a cheeky comment at the crucial moment.

As the boys watched, Coco poked her snout into the scrub. She sniffed. As she picked up the scent, her tail stiffened and she pushed all the way in.

The pheasants exploded from the bushes in a flurry of beating wings and panicked cries, flying vertically into the sky. But Flynn was ready for them. With practised ease he let fly, aiming a few feet in front of the leading pheasant to allow for the time it took his stone to travel across the clearing. It caught the bird squarely in the chest, killing it instantly.

In less a second he had reloaded and was lining up the second bird, now almost at the height of the treetops and flying away rapidly. Just as he was about to fire, he heard a twang, and saw Paddy's arrow streak up and strike the bird. It fell back to earth, and was lost from view behind a low stand of trees.

Flynn turned to Paddy with a quizzical expression.

"It was getting away," said Paddy, a grin plastered across his face.

"No it wasn't," replied Flynn.

"Yes it was."

This could go on for hours. "OK, you win," said Flynn.

Paddy winked at him, which made Flynn laugh.

"Let's eat," said Paddy.

Flynn shook his head in disbelief. His brother was constantly hungry; they had eaten less than an hour ago. But Paddy had already produced a loaf of bread and a flask of honey from his rucksack. Flynn went to retrieve the pheasants while Paddy prepared their lunch.

As he walked up through the clearing, he rose above the level of the forest further down the mountainside. A magnificent view was revealed. The treetops spread out before him in a living avalanche of green, clear to the coast. It was met by the blue of the ocean – a turquoise ring around The Island that gave way to the endless expanse of deeper blue outside the reef. To the east, he could see the dazzling white, snowy peaks of Mt Difficulty and Mt Astonishing. It was paradise on earth.

The first pheasant was easy to find, but Paddy's bird had been moving fast and was somewhere in the thick scrub. He searched for it for a few minutes, but had no luck.

"Coco!" called Flynn. The dog would easily sniff it out. He looked up to see where she was and spotted her further up the hill. She was, as usual, trotting along, nose to the ground, following a thousand fascinating scent trails to see what was at the end of them. Flynn often wondered what it must be like to have such an acute sense of smell — it must be like seeing with your nose, he thought.

Reluctantly she tore herself away, turned in his direction and began heading back down the hill. At the same instant, a shadow passed over Flynn, ghosting across the ground. He looked up, and what he saw made his hair stand on end.

A massive, blood-red dragon sliced silently through the air. It was travelling at a scarcely believable speed, dropping out of the sky like a fiery comet. It took a second for Flynn to judge its direction, before suddenly realising it was heading straight for Coco. The dragon was already extending its huge talons to strike the dog. It would kill Coco instantly.

"COCO!" he screamed, following it up with two short, sharp whistles – the order for the dog to return to him quickly. He saw her respond immediately – she could tell from the urgency in his voice that she was needed right away. She bolted, racing through the scrub as fast as she could go. She had no idea what was bearing down upon her.

Flynn saw the dragon adjust its course. The dog was moving fast, and the dragon had to dive more steeply. In one smooth movement, Flynn pulled a stone from the pouch on his belt and placed it into the pocket of his slingshot. He pulled it back to his cheek and took aim at the dragon. But even as he was about to let fly, he knew it was hopeless. It would be like a gnat biting an elephant – the creature wouldn't even feel it.

Suddenly Flynn had an idea. He adjusted his aim, and breathing out, took his shot. The stone flew true and straight, and Flynn winced as it struck Coco's flank, glancing off her hind leg. The dog yelped loudly, twisting and leaping in pain. She was running so fast that it made her stumble and fall, and she tumbled along the ground, striking a log which pitched her over a little ledge on the mountainside. She fell into a small hollow, landing in the leaf litter at the bottom.

At the same instant, the giant red dragon arrived, its huge talons closing like the jaws of a crocodile. Flynn felt the ground shake as it struck. But where the dog had been, there was now nothing but forest floor. In its talons was nothing more than tree roots and earth.

Coco yelped in fright, leapt to her feet and bolted down the mountain. The dragon swung its monstrous head, its huge jaws gaping open. Each of its teeth were the size of Flynn's knife, and sharp as needles.

But the dog was too quick. She twisted and turned, running in panic down the mountainside.

Flynn heard a whoosh over his head and saw one of Paddy's arrows streaking by. It struck the red dragon's forehead, splintering into matchwood. Flynn followed it up with a shot of his own. He aimed for the dragon's eye, but the dragon saw it coming and simply closed its eyelid. Flynn's stone harmlessly bounced off.

The creature opened its mouth and let forth a roar so terrifyingly loud that Flynn felt like his heart would stop. Then, he turned and ran, screaming for his brother to follow suit.

"Get to the trees!" bellowed Flynn. The lower on the mountainside, the thicker the forest. Flynn had no idea whether the red dragon could follow them in there, but he figured it was their only chance.

He ran as he had never run before. He didn't look back. In front of him, Paddy and Coco smashed their way through the undergrowth.

As Flynn ran, he realised he could hear no sound coming from behind him. Either they were safe, or… He took a look behind, up in the sky. And there, coming down at him like a giant eagle, was the dragon. Flynn threw himself to one side, like a hare being chased by a fox. He hit the ground and rolled over and over. There was a shudder and a tremendous crash as the dragon hit the ground behind him.

Flynn didn't turn, but simply rolled back up onto his feet and took off. Behind him the dragon screamed in frustration and Flynn heard its wings beating hard as it took to the air again. But now the boys were deeper in the forest, and they jinked and weaved through the thickening trees. A quick glance behind told Flynn that they were safe; although the dragon was still up there, hovering above the canopy, even his great strength was no match for the huge tree trunks in this ancient forest.

The boys stayed quiet, keeping low and staying under the cover of the thick clumps of ferns growing among the trees. Finally, thankfully, Flynn could neither see or hear the dragon any more. It had given up the chase.

CHAPTER 2

"**B**ut they could have been killed! We could have lost both of them!"

Paddy lay in bed, wide awake.

His mother's voice could be heard plainly through the wall. For the past hour, he had been listening to his parents argue about what had happened that day. Sometimes they spoke quietly, but occasionally they raised their voices.

"Flynn? Are you awake," he whispered.

"Of course I am," replied his brother. "Shh… I'm trying to hear what they're saying."

The boys had burst in the door that afternoon in a state of high excitement after their close call with the ferocious red dragon. Both were talking at once, and their parents had struggled to make sense of their story until they finally calmed down enough to take turns telling it. Their sweet little sister, Ada, was terrified and excited in equal measure.

Their parents' eyes grew wide when they heard how close they had come to being caught. When they had finished the story, their father whistled.

"You are two lucky boys," said their father. "He doesn't often miss his prey."

"Wait," said Flynn. "He? You know that dragon?"

Their father nodded. "That's Big Red," he explained. "We've often wondered if he was still alive. He was always a loner. He never lived with the others at Dragons' Crater."

He told them that the fierce dragon had lived in his cave near the top of Mt Monstrous for as long as anyone could remember – even their grandparents, who had arrived on the island years before their mother was born.

The boys' mother had been silent through all of this, her eyes down. She was clearly shocked and deeply troubled by their story. She had said little as they ate dinner – fresh fish caught in the lagoon that day by their father, with potatoes, lettuce, cucumber, and tomatoes harvested from the garden. Paddy thought of the two pheasants still on the mountain. Perhaps Big Red had found and eaten them? At least he wasn't having dog for his dinner!

Soon after dessert – poached plums and peaches from the trees in the orchard – their mother sent the children to bed. It was clear she wanted to have a private discussion with their father. Ada complained, but when Flynn offered to read her a story she skipped off to her bedroom with glee.

As soon as the brothers had lain down in their own beds, through the wall Paddy heard his mother say something alarming.

"Perhaps we should leave The Island? I never really gave it much thought before, but it's dangerous here. Maybe we should go to the mainland, send the children to school, make them wear shoes – the things that normal people do."

"I'm not sure you'd survive doing the things normal people do, my love," replied his father. "You've only ever left this island once – and for just one night, remember?"

But his mother was serious. "Are we doing the right thing?" she asked. "Are we putting our own children at risk? Are we responsible parents? I just don't know any more."

There was a long silence while his father thought this over.

"Look," he said. "The boys weren't hurt. And one thing's for certain – they won't go anywhere near the top of Mt Monstrous again. We've taught them well – they're strong, independent, resourceful, and clever. They can read as well as any child from the city.

Yes – there are good things on the mainland that they miss out on – playing sports with friends, riding bikes, going to the cinema. But their life here more than makes up for all of that. Their friends are falcons and horses, dolphins and whales. Their classroom is the wilderness. Occasionally it might be a bit dangerous, yes, but look how good they are at getting themselves out of trouble. Didn't they escape today all on their own?"

Paddy's mother made a joke about having no idea what a cinema was, and then he heard them laugh together. It made him feel better.

"Tell you what," said his father. "How about I sing you a song from my favourite movie? It's called Grease."

Paddy looked over at Flynn in the darkness and saw the light glinting from his teeth and knew he was smiling.

"Oh boy," said Flynn. "Block your ears."

Paddy giggled.

Just then, a soft whinny came from the open window. Paddy looked up to see a long, brown nose, illuminated by the moon, poking through the curtains.

"Clappers," he whispered, standing up on his bed and hugging the horse around her neck. "Have you come to say goodnight?"

Flynn stood up too and stroked the horse's silky nose.

"Hello, girl," he said. "Where's Lightning?"

As if to answer the question, a soft *"squee"* could be heard from the treetops. It was soon followed by a flurry of beating wings, and out of the darkness swooped a falcon, which alighted on Clappers' back and hopped up her neck to stand on her head. The horse didn't mind a bit.

Lightning then hopped onto Flynn's outstretched hand and allowed himself to be patted.

"It's past your bedtime, boy," said Flynn, stroking the speckled brown and white feathers of his breast.

Lightning was content to sleep sitting on the windowsill while Clappers wandered away into the orchard. Paddy lay down again, and his thoughts were of Big Red, up there on the mountainside, alone in his cave. Now that Paddy wasn't so frightened, he could appreciate what a magnificent dragon Big Red was – certainly the biggest on The Island. He was glad to have seen him, no matter how scary it had been. He just hoped his mother could see it that way.

"Night, Flynn," he murmured, closing his eyes, already half asleep.

"Night," Flynn replied.

CHAPTER 3

The next morning, Flynn woke before dawn. Sleepily he turned over. As his eyes adjusted to the gloom, he got a shock to see a large shadowy figure sitting upright on Paddy's bed! Flynn was frozen with fear. Whoever was on his brother's bed was larger than their father. The person had a strange, lumpy head and weirdly rounded shoulders. He sat as still as a stone, which made it all the more spooky. Suddenly the shoulders of the silhouette began to shake, and Flynn heard a giggle he recognised as his brother's. Then the figure's head fell off and landed on the bed, making Paddy laugh out loud.

"Paddy! What the heck!" said Flynn.

His heart was still beating too fast to see the funny side and he had a strong urge to yell at his brother. Paddy was throwing off the rest of the pillows and blankets he had piled up on his head and shoulders to form the eerie figure.

"I started off trying to wake you up using just the power of my mind," whispered Paddy, "but you didn't wake and I got bored, so I decided to spook you instead."

Flynn couldn't help himself; he giggled. Paddy was the undisputed family champion of cracking jokes, which he also happened to laugh at more than anybody else. Sometimes, Paddy literally fell over from laughing so hard at his own jokes. If there was ever an opportunity to play a trick on somebody, Paddy would take it. Over the years, Flynn had endured buckets of freezing water falling on his head, lizards in his shoes, chicken eggs in his hat, and countless other practical jokes dreamed up by his brother.

At the foot of Paddy's bed, Coco whined in her sleep, her legs twitching as though she was running on her side.

"She's dreaming of chasing rabbits again," said Paddy.

"Maybe we should find her some real ones. Want to go exploring?" Flynn asked.

"Of course!" Paddy replied.

The boys silently packed their bags in the darkness, careful not to wake their parents in the next room. They brought the usual things: rope, knives, binoculars, and flint for starting a campfire. Flynn grabbed his slingshot and attached to his belt a small leather bag filled with rounded stones.

Flynn's weapon never left his side. Ever since he could walk, his parents had shown him and his brother how to shoot both the bow and arrow and the slingshot. The boys were experts. As they got older, Paddy naturally began to use the bow and arrow more, and Flynn the slingshot.

His weapon was made from dogwood. He had crafted it himself after finding the perfect Y-shaped piece in the forest. For many hours, he carefully shaved away all the bark, leaving a silky smooth finish. Then, with his mother's help, he had harvested the sap from a rubber tree. He watched her closely, never missing a single step, when she showed him how to make the sap strong and elastic with steam from a pot of water, which boiled all day. The stretchy material made powerful bands that they bound to the forks of the handle. In the centre of the bands, Flynn had attached the small leather pocket that his mother had sewn. Finally, for grip, he had bound the handle with thin flax rope – his weapon was complete.

Flynn became fast at firing the slingshot. He could send five stones high into the air, one after another, before the first one even hit the ground. He and

Paddy liked to compete by snuffing out a lit candle from twenty feet away.

Sneaking through the kitchen, Flynn saw Paddy stuff half a loaf of bread and a small jar of jam into his rucksack before the pair crept out the door. It squeaked loudly on its hinges, making the boys giggle. Coco padded sleepily along behind them.

Outside, Flynn picked a dozen apricots from the tree in the orchard. Their parents had planted many fruit trees, so that no matter what season it was, there was always something tasty to pick.

Paddy gave a low whistle for Clappers. She came trotting up out of the gloom, whinnying softly. The boys made a fuss of her, patting her nose and nuzzling their heads into her warm neck. Flynn leapt up onto her back first, Paddy followed, and soon they were quietly plodding their way through the forest. Lightning came fluttering down out of the trees, settled comfortably on Flynn's shoulder and appeared to go to sleep.

"Nice to see you too," Flynn said to the bird.

Three hours later, the brothers were deep in dense forest, on a plateau high above the Eastern Bays of the island. They walked silently through the undergrowth, with Coco following just a few paces behind. The dog was alert now and excitedly sniffing the breeze. A few minutes earlier they had turned Clappers out onto a meadow where she happily chomped the lush, sweet grass. When the boys were hunting, Clappers' hooves made far too much noise.

From high above, Lightning gave a squawk. Paddy suddenly held up a hand, and both Flynn and Coco stopped in their tracks. Paddy pointed to the top of the ridge. He stretched two fingers on each hand and brought them to either side of his forehead, letting Flynn know that he had spotted a deer. Flynn crept through the trees until he got a clear look; It was a young stag, with a fine set of antlers.

The brothers, keeping low, quietly walked around in a broad semicircle until they were directly downwind of the deer, so that it couldn't trace their scent on the wind.

Paddy then pulled an arrow from his quiver, and skilfully notched it on the string of his bow. Flynn took three stones from his pouch and placed one in his slingshot. The other two he put into his mouth, tucking them inside his cheek. Whenever he went to the beach, he kept an eye out for the perfect stones for his slingshot. They were as smooth as could be, ground that way by the ceaseless action of the waves. He collected them always, and stored them in the leather pouch on his belt.

When they were hunting, Flynn and Paddy took turns. Now it was Paddy's turn to shoot first, but Flynn was ready with a stone should his brother miss the target.

"If you miss you're a rotten egg," whispered Flynn. Although it sounded more like "Fff y mss rohheneg" because of the stones in his cheek.

Paddy clamped his lips, obviously trying not to laugh, and ducked under a branch. He was now close enough to take a shot. Flynn watched as his brother steadied his breathing and drew the arrow back to its full length. He closed one eye, and looked along the arrow to take aim. Loosening his fingers on the bow string, he prepared to let fly.

Suddenly, sensing danger, the deer raised its head. A tenth of a second later, it was running at top speed along the ridge, heading towards the sea. Paddy loosed an arrow, but it missed its mark.

"Gfff! Arrr!" yelled Flynn, sprinting after the deer. As he ran, he drew back his slingshot. The thick forest was making it difficult to get a clear shot, and the deer disappeared behind tree trunks and leapt high in the air.

Finally Flynn got his chance, and sent a stone hurtling after it. He would have hit the deer had it not run behind a large tree at that very moment.

The stone thudded into the trunk and fell harmlessly to the ground.

By the time the boys reached the spot where they had last seen the deer it was long gone, having disappeared into the thick forest covering the hillside. Coco had given chase, but a dog was no match for the speed of a panicked deer.

"You took so long to take that shot! I thought you must have fallen asleep," laughed Flynn.

Paddy responded by glaring at his brother. He was clearly annoyed he had missed.

Flynn looked out to sea. It was a magical view. It was so clear he could see straight to the bottom, the clumps of seaweed and coral, and the lighter blue of the twisting channels. The treacherous path through the coral on this side of the island was so difficult to navigate that it had come to be known as the Gulp Swallow Pass.

He looked further to the west, to the calm cove inside the reef, where the surface of the water was so still and clear it was like there was no sea at all.

What he saw made his blood run cold.

He tried to call out, but no sound would come.
Instead he simply pointed, his body rigid with fright. His
mouth hung open. Finally, with great effort, he spoke.

"Paddy – look!"

Paddy had just finished putting his arrows neatly
back into his quiver, and he rushed over and stood by
Flynn's side. Together, they looked out into the bay.

There, anchored inside the reef, was a sleek black
boat. It was large and low – built for high speeds.
On the side of it was the image of a white dog – its
mouth open, its sharp teeth bared in an ugly snarl.

CHAPTER 4

Flynn had seen that white dog before, painted onto the side of a black plane.

He had first spotted the plane about a month back, on a perfect blue-sky day. His sharp ears had caught the buzzing sound of the engine before it came into view.

"What's that?" he had called to Paddy. His brother was busy digging a hole in the sandy beach so large and deep their entire family could have stood in it.

"What's what?" said Paddy, looking up. He was sweating and puffing from his work. Sand stuck to every part of his body. His face was covered in bits of shell and sand.

"That!" Flynn yelled impatiently. "Can't you hear it?" The noise of the engine was getting louder.

"Hey!" shouted Paddy. "I hear something. Can you hear that?"

At that moment a small plane had flown over the top of the forest, low enough to make the boys jump. They dived into the bottom of Paddy's hole, frightened they might be hit! It had taken Flynn a moment to realise what it was – he'd never seen a plane that close before, but only as tiny little dots miles up in the sky, completely silent, with white trails streaming out behind them like spiders' silk.

Flynn had gotten a good look at it as it passed overhead. It was glossy black, with a white dog's head painted on the door. It travelled at great speed. The noise of its propellers was terrific.

That day, the plane had flown over the sea, turned, and headed for the mainland.

The next week, it had happened again. Two days later, they saw it again, further to the west. Before long, the boys saw it flying over the island almost every day – sometimes high in the sky, sometimes skimming the tree tops.

Whenever it had come especially close to their house, their parents walked outside to watch it fly by, before turning to each other with a worried expression on their faces.

One day, Flynn noticed that there were two men sitting behind the pilot. They were each holding something tubular and black, which they pointed out of the windows.

Once, when the plane had flown low over their house, Paddy ran outside, picked up a stone, and hurled it with all his might. Flynn could see the surprise on the pilot's face as the stone whizzed past him, just inches from the windscreen.

Then, just like that, the plane didn't show up again. Flynn was glad to see it go – the constant noise of the engine irritated him.

The peace of the island had returned. No sounds could be heard, other than the usual ones – the twitter of birds, the occasional snort of an animal in the forest, and the distant roar of the surf breaking on the outer reef.

Life had returned to normal... until now, thought Flynn, as he gazed at the boat floating in the bay, a panicky feeling in his chest.

CHAPTER 5

P addy used the tip of his bow to slowly part the long, sword-like leaves of the flax so they could get a clear view. For a long time, neither brother spoke, but simply stared at the black boat floating in the bay.

"How on earth did they find their way through the Gulp Swallow Pass?" asked Flynn.

Paddy could think of no answer. To see a strange boat anchored in the bay was such an astonishingly unusual sight that he couldn't take his eyes from it.

Then, Paddy noticed something further along the beach. It was a much smaller boat – a dinghy – pulled up onto the sand. Whoever had arrived in the large boat had come to shore in the dinghy and was now nowhere to be seen. He nudged Flynn, and pointed at it.

"Come with me," said Flynn.

Paddy pulled back into the cover of the trees, away from the beach. For a few minutes, he followed his brother in silence, until he felt mud squelching under his feet.

"Where are we going?" he asked.

"To collect some reeds," said Flynn.

Paddy understood immediately. He began to look around for the tall plants that grew in the wetlands and swamps on The Island. Before long, they came across a patch and set about cutting the reed stalks into pieces as long as their forearms.

The reeds were stiff and hollow and strong for such a lightweight plant. Once they had collected a handful of them, they set off again for the beach.

Back in the cover of the flax, they laid down their bags and weapons. Flynn told Coco to lie down. Obediently, the dog curled up under a bush and was still. "Stay," he commanded.

A shallow stream wound its way down from the hills and emptied into the bay. The boys slipped into it on their bellies. Sinking their heads and bodies below the surface, they pulled themselves along the bottom. They held their breath as they worked their way downstream. If anyone was watching from the beach, they wouldn't see the boys under the water as they made their way into the sea.

Paddy knew they had reached the ocean when he tasted salt water. Flipping onto their backs, the brothers put a reed into their mouths and raised it above the surface. They breathed through them as easily and naturally as breathing through a snorkel. If one of the reeds leaked, they simply replaced it with another of the spares they brought

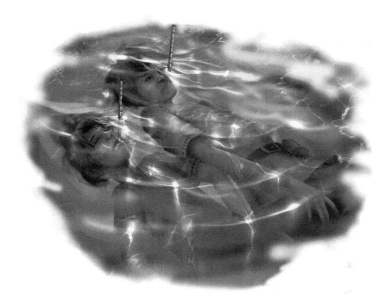

along with them – without ever having to come to the surface for air.

Together, the boys made their way further out into the cove until they reached the black boat. Anyone watching would think it was simply a half-submerged log with some of its branches sticking up out of the water.

They broke the surface only when they reached the seaward side of the boat.

Without a sound they bobbed in the water, silent as two sharks, listening for any sign that someone was aboard. The boat was even bigger up close. It was long and sleek, coated in glossy black paint, apart from the dog's snarling face. Up front, the boys could see that there were sleeping quarters and a large indoor cabin. At the stern of the boat was a wide wooden deck. Underneath, two huge propellers hung down into the water.

Suddenly, from inside the cabin, Paddy heard a crackling sound, followed by a man's voice. It sounded strange, like it was coming through a long pipe. The boys pulled themselves as far under the hull of the boat as possible… and listened.

"Ground crew. Come in, ground crew, over. Stand by for instructions. Printing now."

The voice went quiet. In its place came another sound. *Click! Click! Whirr!* Then, nothing.

The boys stayed in the water for five anxious minutes, listening. There wasn't another sound. All that could be heard was the water lapping gently against the hull. Paddy looked at Flynn, who nodded. Silently, Paddy pulled himself up and over the stern. He was ready to dive back into the water at the slightest sound or movement. There was none.

"Come on up," he said to Flynn.

Once inside, Paddy just stood and stared, dripping water on the floor. He couldn't believe his eyes. There was so much stuff he had never seen before. On the table sat a large square black screen. Under that was a small unit with rows of buttons, each of which had either a letter of the alphabet or a number on it. He had no idea what it could be. Beside it was a box, which had a blinking light on it. A sheet of paper was poking out of it. The sheet had strange markings on it, like it might be some kind of writing, but he couldn't make any sense of it. The markings were curious, some curved like fishhooks, others simply straight lines. At the bottom were two words he could read: The Pitbull. He wondered what it meant.

He concentrated on the symbols, trying to figure out what each might mean. It was impossible, and he soon gave up. There were several other pages scattered around on the table top, each with a strange picture on it.

On the seat lay a small leather purse. He flipped it over a few times to examine it. Then, he unfolded it and looked in its little pockets. In one of them he found a colourful piece of paper, with some pictures and the number fifty on it. He suddenly realised what it was.

"Hey Flynn, look. This must be money."

Flynn came over to see. "I guess so," he replied.

Paddy considered the note for a while, wondering why on earth anyone would swap this piece of paper for anything. Then, he went back to his exploration of the cabin. Scattered in the kitchen were lots of little packets and sealed tubular tins, each with a glossy image on it. In surprise he realised that they contained food! What a strange way to eat, he thought.

"Coca Cola," said Flynn.

Paddy turned around. His brother was reading

from the side of a red and white tin, with a little white tube coming out of a hole in the top. He sniffed it warily.

"Smells weird," said Flynn. "Perhaps it's for cleaning."

Paddy looked out of the window, checking for the dinghy. Still there. Then he noticed a strange object on the window ledge. It looked like two mirrored eyes, at the sides of which protruded short, curved arms. As he turned them over in his hand, all of a sudden he realised what to do with them, and slid them onto his face, looking through the small glass panes. The cabin instantly became darker.

"Hey Flynn. Look at me!"

Flynn turned around and jumped when he saw Paddy.

"What the heck, Paddy!" he said, laughing. "You look weird."

Paddy grinned, and took them off. "They make it hard to see," he said. As he spoke, he saw Flynn's expression suddenly change.

"It's us," said Flynn, pointing.

Paddy spun around to see what had given him such a fright. A shiver ran down his spine. Tacked to the wall were ten large photos. It seemed they were taken from above – he guessed from the plane. In three of them, the boys were standing on the beach, with their parents in the background by the house. Their mother had a worried expression on her face, and she held tightly onto their sister, Ada.

Paddy had never seen photos of himself before.

"How…" he began, but his voice trailed off.

"This is bad," said Flynn. "I don't like it at all."

Paddy pulled a photo of himself from the wall and looked closely at it.

"Oh well. I guess they know we're here," he said. "Look at the hole I dug that day. That was a great hole."

He pinned it back on the wall.

"Let's go," said Flynn. "We need to get home and tell Mum and Dad."

"Just a few more minutes," said Paddy. "Whoa! Have a look at this!"

He had picked up a black device, a little larger, but thinner, than a pack of cards. When he pushed a button at the bottom of it, the screen lit up to reveal rows of little coloured squares. He almost dropped it in surprise.

"I've never seen anything like it. What is it?" he said to Flynn.

"I don't know," replied Flynn, who came closer to look. "Is it hot? Look at all those colours!"

Paddy turned it over to see if any light came from the back. It was flat and smooth with a little hole in the top corner. When he flipped it back again, the light disappeared and the screen went black.

"Oh no," said Flynn. "It's gone out."

Paddy prodded the button again, and the colourful squares reappeared.

"What happens if you touch one of them?" asked Flynn.

Paddy responded by tapping on a reddish square with the letters 'AR' on it.

"Let's see," he said.

Paddy waited a few seconds, and then gasped as the screen suddenly showed a picture of what was directly behind the device. He pointed it at the sea, and there, on the screen, was the sea. He pointed it at the sky. On the screen, was the sky. Paddy pointed it at his brother.

"Woah! You're ugly!" he said to Flynn, who poked out his tongue.

Paddy walked around the cabin pointing the device at everything he could see. Eventually he found himself back at the table. Flynn was studying the piece of paper that had come out of the box on the table. Paddy held the device over the sheet. Then, something incredible happened. On the screen of the device, the strange markings on the paper started to move, growing into something different.

"Flynn! Look at this!" exclaimed Paddy. Flynn looked at the screen. Before his eyes, the markings transformed, turning into letters, and the letters into a message. Paddy moved the device to the side and looked again at the paper. But, the markings remained the same – completely unreadable. Again, he held the device over the paper. Quite clearly, the words reappeared. As he read them, he felt suddenly sick.

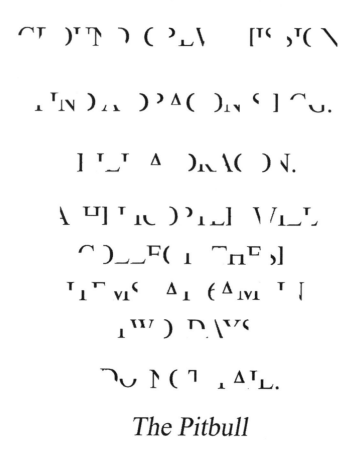

The Pitbull

Here's your first opportunity to use the **AR Reads** app on your device (if you haven't downloaded it, you can find the instructions at the beginning of this book).

Simply start up the app, then point the device at this page and watch as the code reveals itself! If you don't have a device – don't worry – just read on!

"Ground crew mission," read Paddy. "Find a dragon's egg. Kill a dragon. A helicopter will collect these items at 6am in two days. Do not fail. The Pitbull."

He was in complete shock, and it was a moment before he could speak.

"This is so bad," he simply said.

Flynn nodded.

"I guess now we know for sure there are still dragons on the island," he said. "But how did these people find out?"

"They must have seen them from their plane," guessed Paddy. A lump had formed in his throat.

CHAPTER 6

"What are we going to do?" Paddy asked. The boys stood in the cabin of the black boat. Flynn suddenly felt very afraid. He tried to calm down, forcing himself to think clearly.

"Well, we need to do something quickly," he said. "The instructions said to find a dragon's egg. Perhaps we could try to find the dragon's eggs first and move them?"

Paddy shook his head.

"That's not going to work," he said. "They must weigh a tonne. Even Clappers couldn't move one. And what about the next part, where it says to kill a dragon? Who is this Pitbull character anyway? I'll fire an arrow into his butt."

Just as Paddy said the word "butt", Flynn heard a shout and a faint splash.

Keeping low, he and Paddy ran out of the cabin and onto the back deck.

The dinghy – with three men in it – was already half way back to the boat! It was the strangest thing, seeing other people on the island, and for a second Flynn forgot about the terrible risk they were taking by being there. The men were all wearing black tee shirts, black trousers, and heavy black boots. There, on the front of their black caps, was the white dog with the sharp teeth.

One man stood up in the rear of the dinghy. He was short and powerfully built. Even from the boat

Flynn could see the large knife in his belt.

A second man, tall and wiry, rowed the boat. But, it was the third man, a giant with bulging muscles, who truly frightened the boys. He kneeled in the front of the dinghy and bared his yellow broken teeth. Flynn could tell he was the leader – he rudely yelled for the boat to go faster.

"We have to go," said Flynn. "Quickly!"

"It's too late. If we dive off now they'll see us," Paddy replied.

Flynn ran back inside, dragging Paddy with him. Together they looked around the cabin, desperate for an idea.

Flynn ran into the bedroom up the front of the boat. They needed an escape plan, and fast! Every second, the men were closer to discovering them on their boat. He suddenly saw a way out. Above him, in the ceiling, he spotted a hatch which opened up onto the deck.

"Paddy!" he called. "Look. We can get out here!"

Paddy examined it.

"Good thinking," he said. "But we're going to have to wait until they're actually on board before we climb out of it, or else they'll see us. I'll unclip it so we can open it quickly."

Together, the boys waited silently beneath the hatch, listening to the creak of the oars as the boat came closer. Flynn could hear the men talking.

"We'll collect the last of the gear," said one. "Then we can go and get the egg, shoot the first dragon we see and get the hell off this horrible island."

"Horrible is right. I don't know what The Pitbull was thinking, sending us here," said another.

"Think about it, you idiots."

Flynn figured this voice was the leader's.

"No one in the world has a dragon. No one even believes that they're real. If The Pitbull can hatch a live one in his private zoo, he's going to make himself a whole pile of money. He can charge people whatever he wants to come and see it."

One of the other men moaned. "I've never seen his private zoo."

"Me neither," said the other. "What's in it?"

"That's because the two of you are pond scum. Why would he invite you? In that zoo there's just about every earthly creature that could hurt or kill a person. Tigers, deadly snakes, crocodiles, poisonous spiders, Tasmanian devils, scorpions. The Pitbull even has a box jellyfish, a blue-ringed octopus, and a great white shark in a tank."

The men were tying the dinghy to the back of the boat. Flynn looked at Paddy; he had one hand on the hatch.

"Why does he want a dead dragon?" said one of the men.

"He's going to stuff it and display it in his house," replied the leader. Through the open door of the cabin Flynn could see the men clambering out of the dinghy.

On the bed, directly below the hatch, was a plastic bag – just another thing Flynn had never seen before. He picked it up and rubbed it between his fingers. He pulled it from each end, testing its strength. An idea suddenly formed in his mind.

Without a word to his brother he sprinted back out into the main cockpit.

"Flynn!" hissed Paddy. "What are you doing?! We need to go – now!"

But Flynn ignored him. With lightening speed, and in silence, he gathered up all the papers on the table in the cockpit. On his way back to the bedroom he grabbed the phone from where Paddy had left it.

Paddy looked at him, astonished.

"Are you crazy?"

But Flynn took no notice. He quickly shoved the papers and the phone into the plastic bag and tied it tightly in a knot at the top.

"Go," he said to Paddy. "Go!"

The men had now crossed the back deck and were walking into the cabin. As quickly and quietly as he could, Paddy lifted the hatch and jumped up through it. Flynn passed him the bag and followed, hoping the men didn't see his feet disappearing through the ceiling.

The boys heard an angry shout.

"Which one of you numbskulls left the hatch open? What if it had rained? I'll skin you both alive if my bed gets wet."

On the deck, the boys prepared to leap off the side. Flynn knew they'd have to dive as straight as an arrow to make the smallest possible splash. They couldn't risk the men hearing them escape. Luckily, both boys had practised this a thousand times.

Together, they drew in a huge breath and dived, entering the water at exactly the same time. They made barely a ripple, when Flynn turned on his back he could just make out the lone figure of a man on deck, looking out across the bay. Thankfully he didn't look down.

Ten feet under, Flynn and Paddy swam towards the shore, careful not to blow any bubbles.

They moved slowly to conserve their breath.

The plastic bag worked beautifully, keeping the papers and the phone dry. The man had given up and gone back inside long before the boys eventually surfaced, almost at the shore.

CHAPTER 7

"**W**hat are we going to do with this?" asked Paddy, holding up the plastic bag. Coco was sniffing it with interest.

"They're going to come looking for it, you know," he continued, but Flynn held up his hand to stop him talking.

"I'm thinking," he said.

"Well, think faster," replied Paddy. "I think they've just figured out that their stuff is missing!" From across the water angry shouts could be heard.

Suddenly, the men were on the deck of the boat! All three looked towards the shore. Even from this distance Paddy could tell they were furious. The two boys shrank down into the flax.

"Keep still," hissed Flynn.

Without warning the leader erupted with a bellow, struck one of the other men across the head and stalked back inside.

"Let's go," said Paddy. The two boys ran as quickly as they could back to Clappers.

They rode the horse hard, until a thick layer of foamy sweat appeared on her back. Just before their home came into view, Flynn slowed Clappers to a walk. He turned to Paddy.

"We can't say anything to Mum and Dad."

"Why not?" Paddy asked.

"Because if Dad finds out about those men, he'll find them and tell them to leave the island. They might try to hurt him."

Paddy nodded, his mouth in a grim line.

"Then what can we do?"

"Those men don't have a horse, so they won't be able to make it here before dark," said Flynn. "I think we'll be safe tonight. For now, we keep quiet. Later, we can look at the rest of this stuff and see what we can figure out. Tomorrow, we take action."

"What kind of action?" asked Paddy.

"I don't know," Flynn replied. "But we're going to have to be clever, and very brave."

CHAPTER 8

The boys were unusually quiet that night while eating their dinner.

"When I saw that you were gone this morning I thought we might have some fresh rabbit or venison for dinner. Instead, you come home with a whole lot of fresh air," teased their mother.

"Hooray for Ada!" shouted their sister. Their parents smiled. With only a little bit of help from her father, she had caught two large fish on a hand line from the beach that afternoon. Now the family was enjoying them for dinner.

"Hooray for Ada!" they all shouted, and Paddy tickled her tummy.

After dinner, Paddy helped to do the clearing up while Flynn read Ada a bedtime story. She snuggled up beside him while he read, trying to make the story exciting for her. Then she walked around the house singing and demanding a butterfly kiss from everyone, including Coco. Sometimes she made the whole family laugh even more than Paddy did. Finally, she climbed into bed and was asleep in seconds.

Flynn could see his parents were amazed when a few minutes later he announced that they, too, were tired and off to bed.

"Are you boys feeling all right?" asked their father, disappointed. He was shuffling a deck of cards and Flynn could see he was just about to challenge his sons to a game. He gave them a searching look.

"Just tired, that's all," said Paddy. He yawned theatrically.

"Night night, then," said their mum, and kissed their heads. "Sleep tight, my lovely boys."

It was only when Flynn heard his parents go to bed that he felt it was safe to bring out the plastic bag containing the papers and the phone.

There were five sheets of paper, one of which had the strange markings on it, and the others had only a simple picture.

There was a picture of the points of a compass with a dragon's skull in the centre.

Another showed a sketch of an oval shape, with a baby dragon curled up inside. Without doubt, it was a dragon's egg.

A third sheet had eight arrows pointing in different directions.

A final sheet of paper had a picture of a strange-looking contraption on it – a black device with a handle on top and a glass bulb like a fish eye at one end.

"What strange pictures," said Paddy. "What do they mean?"

"I have a feeling the only way to find out is to use this," said Flynn, holding up the phone.

"Ah ha!" said Paddy. "I've been waiting ages for you to figure that out."

Flynn smiled.

"Let's start with this one," he said, holding up the sheet of paper with the picture of the compass points on it.

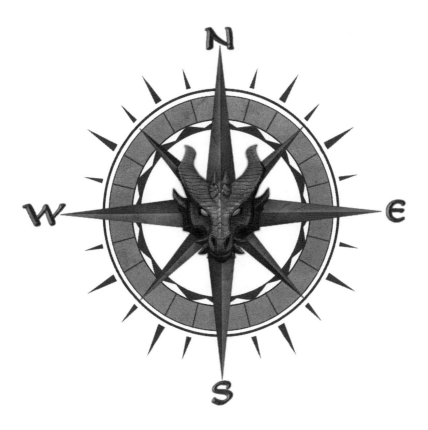

Here's your second opportunity to use the **AR Reads** app on your device (if you haven't downloaded it, you can find the instructions at the beginning of this book).

Simply start up the app, then point the device at this page and discover just how the men made it past the razor reef to the island. If you don't have a device – don't worry – just keep reading!

"Hey! That's our island!" yelled Paddy.

"Shhh!" hissed Flynn. "You'll wake Mum and Dad!"

They huddled together to look at the screen of the phone. Flynn instantly recognised a bird's-eye view of their island. He'd never seen it from this angle – it was truly beautiful to look at. Then, dropping down through the clouds, the screen showed the detail of the reef up close. They could clearly see the twisty path through the coral and rocks – it was deeper water, with a white, sandy bottom, and therefore lighter than the surrounding coral. Then, the black boat appeared on the screen. It was moving. It began outside the reef and began to make its way through the channel.

"That's the Gulp Swallow Pass!" Paddy exclaimed. "That's how they made it through without wrecking their boat!"

"Will you be quiet!" replied Flynn. "They must have been mapping the reef when they were flying over in the plane."

Flynn thought about how difficult it was to pass through the reef surrounding The Island. It was the main reason that no other people outside of their family had ever lived on it. No one was crazy enough to try and steer a boat through the incredibly complicated maze of coral and rocks. No one, that is, but their parents. And, of course, their grandmother. It instantly made him think of his grandparents. They turned up on the island each and every month without fail, and always the next day after the full moon. Paddy and Flynn liked to keep their curtains wide open so they could search for the moon out of the bedroom window. They'd count down the days until finally the full moon appeared in the sky. In the morning the boys would rush down to the beach and train their father's binoculars out to sea. For hours they'd search the horizon, looking for the tiny bright white triangle – the sail of their grandparents' little yacht. As they approached the island, their grandmother would stand at the helm of the yacht, with one hand on the wheel and the other shielding her eyes from the glare. Calmly, she'd steer the yacht through the reef. It was a narrow and twisty pass, sometimes looping back on itself. At one point, they had to steer a figure-of-eight just to squeeze through. The boys had named it Granny's Pass.

Flynn smiled as he thought of his grandfather. He was the complete opposite. He'd scamper from one side of the boat to the other. He'd peer over the edge, pointing at the sharpest bits and shouting loudly to his wife to "watch out for Heaven's sake!" She ignored absolutely everything he said. When finally the yacht would arrive in the calm cove just out from their home, their grandfather would yell "Hallelujah!" while their grandmother would give one of her knowing smiles and wink at the boys waiting on the beach.

Flynn loved his grandparents' visits more than anything else. They always brought with them books and more books. Sometimes, they were wonderful tales of adventure – life on the high seas, the polar ice caps, or the high mountains. Other times, they were stories of children who were sent to stay with evil relatives but managed to escape and have the most brilliant lives.

For days, the brothers would lie in the hammock with their grandparents, while they all read to each other. Through these stories, Flynn was transported to unimaginable places – the grimy streets of Victorian London, the hot sands of the Sahara desert or the ferocious hurricanes of the South Pacific Ocean. It made him feel like he wasn't missing anything of the world.

When they got hot, or had enough of reading for a while, they'd all go for a swim. Sometimes their grandmother would teach them to sail the yacht outside the reef.

In the evenings, there would be special meals cooked by their mother. Afterwards, there was always a family party, and their grandfather would bring out his violin and play old folk songs and teach them all the words.

Flynn thought of how his grandparents had discovered the island when they were young. It was one of his favourite stories.

After they were married, the first thing they did was to start building a yacht in the front garden. For six months they spent every spare moment sawing, drilling, hammering, and gluing the boat's hull. For six months more they stitched sails, braided ropes, attached pulleys and cleats and a million and one other little jobs.

They had little money, so everything had to be free, or at least very cheap. They spent two days in the forest looking for the perfect tree for their mast. It then took them another whole day to drag it out of the forest with the help of a strong donkey.

The boys' grandfather would sneak out at night to break off chunks of the tarseal road. Bringing them home under the cover of darkness, he would melt them down and spread the sticky tar all over the bottom of the yacht to make it waterproof. In the morning nothing would remain but a freshly tarred hull.

His grandparents told him that when the yacht was finally finished, it was towed down to the wharf and carefully lowered into the water. A bottle of milk was smashed on its prow for good luck. The very next day, the couple set off to explore the big wide world.

But they had only sailed five hundred miles when a big storm blew them off course. All night they battled the shrieking winds and lashing rain. However, it wasn't enough.

As morning arrived they could see they were being blown directly towards the deadly reef surrounding an island. His grandmother fought against the storm from the helm, while her husband furiously pulled on ropes and reefed sails. By some miracle they were washed over the first line of rocks and reef, only to be smashed into the second.

Suddenly there was a big hole in the bottom of the boat, and water gushing in! There was no going home.

It took all the skill of the boys' grandmother to bring the half-sunken yacht through the maze of rocks and coral to the beach. Eventually she succeeded, and the pair flopped upon the sand and kissed it, grateful to be alive. Flynn could only imagine how isolated they felt.

It took almost three months to repair the damage to their yacht, using only what they could find on the beach or in the forest. With their food supplies ruined by the salt water, the couple survived on nuts and berries for a few days, and then began to hunt for game and catch fish in the cove. By the time their boat was seaworthy, they had grown quite used to living off the land.

The boys' grandparents had also fallen in love with the peace and beauty of The Island. They returned many times over the years, each time bringing with them a load of wood planks, or some sheets of glass, or iron for the roof of the small home they built there – the home in which Flynn and Paddy now lived.

But now, Flynn realised, not even the razor reef could keep their family safe.

Suddenly, a thought struck him.

"Now that we have their secret map," he said to Paddy, "how are they going to get their boat back out again?"

CHAPTER 9

"Listen! Did you hear that? I think there's someone outside," said Flynn.

The boys had been discussing how to get rid of three very dangerous and angry men. Paddy was suddenly gripped with terror.

"They couldn't possibly have made it here by now – and in the dark," he said, but he didn't feel so sure.

"Blow out the candle," hissed Flynn. With a puff Paddy plunged the room into darkness.

Through the open window Paddy heard a loud snap, like a twig breaking underfoot.

Flynn didn't hesitate. In one smooth movement he rolled out of bed, while at the same time grabbing up his slingshot and a stone from the bedside table. In less than a second he was standing at the window, his slingshot drawn back to his cheek. His arm shook with fear. Paddy looked at him; he worried that the shaking might make Flynn miss whoever was outside. Paddy stood beside him.

Now came a rustle of dry grass right outside the window!

"On the count of three, pull back the curtain – quickly," whispered Flynn.

Paddy nodded in silence, and swallowed hard.

"One," said Flynn. "Two. Three!"

Paddy whipped the curtain open and Flynn prepared to let fly at the intruder. In the darkness Paddy saw a face looming! As it came closer, the face grew longer. And browner. And hairier! Suddenly it gave a loud whinny and a warm grassy smell filled the open window.

"Clappers! You crazy horse! You scared us half to death!" laughed Paddy with relief. Flynn lowered his slingshot, shaking his head. The boys stroked the horse's nose through the window.

"I guess we're a bit jumpy. You keep a lookout, Clappers. There's a good horse," said Flynn.

Clappers soon grew hungry and wandered away to graze.

"Let's try another of these pictures," suggested Paddy. "What about this one?" He held up the picture of the black device with the handle at the top and the fish eye at the end.

"That's the one that must have come out of the machine when we were swimming outside the boat – the one we heard," said Flynn.

"So it's the most recent," said Paddy.

Paddy picked up the device and tapped at the bottom to light up the screen.

"That's weird," said Paddy.

"What is?" asked Flynn.

"See here, up in the corner. There's a rectangle that used to be half-coloured-in white. Now it's only a tiny bit coloured-in, and has turned red."

Flynn came over to look.

"Hmm. I didn't notice that before."

"That's because I'm so much smarter than you," said Paddy. "What do you think it means?"

"You tell me, since you're so smart," replied Flynn.

Paddy was silent for a moment, then shrugged his shoulders. He laid the sheet of paper with the drawing on his bed, tapped on the 'AR' button on the phone, and held it over the paper.

You can use the **AR Reads** app on your device to unlock this video. Simply start up the app, then point the device at this page and meet The Pitbull in person. Be warned – he isn't pretty! If you don't have a device – don't worry – just read on!

When a man appeared on the screen the two boys jumped in fright. Paddy even took a quick look behind the phone in case a tiny man was sitting there on the bed.

The man was eating from a large bone, tearing the meat off with his teeth and chewing with slow satisfaction. A horrible scar ran down one side of his face.

The man began to speak. His cold, calm voice made Paddy's hair stand on end. As he spoke, his face began to screw up and he grew angrier. Paddy quickly realised that he must be the men's boss – the one they called The Pitbull.

The message to his men was loud and clear. He wanted his instructions carried out quickly and successfully, with no mistakes… or else!

But it was when he mentioned the boys' family that a chill of fear ran through Paddy.

"If that stupid little family tries to get in your way, or stop you, I think you know what to do," said

The Pitbull, coldly. An evil smile played on his lips.

No sooner had The Pitbull finished delivering his frightening message when the screen of the phone suddenly went black. No amount of tapping on it would make it light up again.

CHAPTER 10

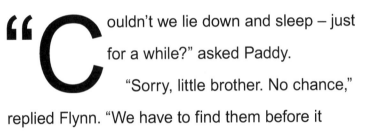

"Couldn't we lie down and sleep – just for a while?" asked Paddy.

"Sorry, little brother. No chance," replied Flynn. "We have to find them before it gets light."

The boys had been stumbling over hills, across rivers and through thick forest for most of the night.

After watching the evil video message from The Pitbull, Flynn had realised how much danger they were in. And not just themselves, but their whole family! They made the decision to leave right away.

They needed to track down the men before they came any closer to their home.

Just what they were going to do when they found them he hadn't the foggiest idea.

The brothers had quietly gathered their weapons in the dark, taken some food, and slipped out of the house. Their parents would think they had left early to go hunting again.

Outside, Flynn had stopped suddenly. He ran back into their bedroom, gathered up the papers, folded them and put them in his pocket. He didn't bother with the dead device.

Much as they had wanted to, they couldn't bring Clappers. She would make too much noise in the forest. They couldn't risk having the men hear them approach.

However, Lightning had appeared from nowhere and settled in on Paddy's shoulder for the journey. Coco was full of excitement about leaving in the middle of the night. She was either getting under the boys' feet or running off to snuffle in the bushes. It made Flynn feel better that they weren't alone.

When they reached a clearing in the forest, it was suddenly quite bright – the clouds had parted to reveal the moon.

"Look – it's full!" said Paddy in excitement.

It had already occurred to Flynn that his grandparents would be out on the ocean, right now, one of them asleep in their bunk, the other keeping watch, while their little yacht sailed through the night towards the island. Then he thought of the men, and realised that now even more of his family would be in danger.

"Yes," said Flynn. "They'll arrive tomorrow."

"Oh, no," said Paddy.

"We need to keep those men well away," nodded Flynn. "There's no other way. We must hurry – we don't have much time." He pointed to the east, where the sky had begun to lighten. The sun would soon be up.

Paddy nodded and began to move his weary legs again.

"How on earth are we going to find them?" he said, but all of a sudden his face lit up.

"Flynn?"

"Yes?"

"If Lightning can find animals for us to hunt, couldn't he help us find the men?"

"Good thinking," said Flynn. "Let's try it."

Paddy tickled the bird's stomach. He was in a deep sleep, yet perfectly balanced on his shoulder. He gave him a little shake and the falcon's eyes flicked open.

"He looks a bit grumpy," said Paddy.

"He sure does," agreed Flynn.

The two boys kept prodding Lightning until the bird was fully awake. Flynn held out his finger and the bird stepped onto it.

"Here's hoping this works," he said. Paddy pursed his lips and gave three short whistles – low to high-pitched – the signal for Lightning to hunt. With a quick motion Flynn flicked the bird up into the air. Within two seconds the falcon had flown up and out of sight. For three whole minutes the boys listened in complete silence, but there was not a sound to be heard apart from some crickets chirping in the grass.

"Well, that was a terrible idea," said Paddy. "I bet he's flown straight home to bed."

Flynn gloomily agreed, and together the boys plunged back into the forest. They tried to walk as quietly as they could, but because they were so tired and the light was so poor, they kept stumbling. Another hour passed, and the light began to filter down into the dark forest. It was morning.

The boys stopped to drink from their flasks.

"It's hopeless," said Paddy. "This is like looking for a needle in a haystack. They could be anywhere."

Just as Paddy finished speaking, the boys heard a faint *'squee!'* from above.

"Did you hear that?" asked Flynn excitedly.

"Yes! I think it's Lightning!"

"It could be another falcon," reasoned Flynn.

"I bet it's Lightning. Come on – it came from that direction."

The boys broke into a jog. Despite his tiredness, Flynn's senses were now fully alert. The boys ran carefully, stepping across logs and making sure not to break any branches. They were as silent as its possible to be when running through the forest.

'Squee!' came the call again, and the boys changed to a new direction, following the falcon. *'Squee, squee, squee!'* Three short calls meant they were very close. Flynn was sure it was Lightning now – they had done this many times when they were hunting.

"Let's just hope it isn't a deer," whispered Flynn.

Suddenly Coco let out a low growl. Paddy put his hand on her head to settle her.

They slowed to a walk, and bent lower to the ground. They moved carefully through the shrubs and ferns that grew on the forest floor.

Suddenly, there was the faint smell of smoke.

The boys had found what they were looking for.

CHAPTER 11

The men looked cold, tired and grumpy after spending the night out in the open. The leader – who the other men called Scorpion – was furiously scratching his bottom. Paddy guessed he had unwittingly slept beside a nest of army ants and forgotten to bring any insect repellant. Red marks covered his arms and legs.

"Those boys are going to pay dearly for stealing our stuff," he raged. "This wasn't part of the plan."

"How do you know it was them?" said the shorter,

stockier man. The others called him Scar. "We didn't catch a glimpse of them, after all."

"There's no one else on the island, you idiot," said the tall, wiry one.

"Listen carefully Spike – if you speak to me like that again I'll knock you as cold as a mackerel," replied Scar.

"He's right," said Scorpion. "You're even stupider than you look. Of course it was them."

Scar remained silent, sulking.

"There's just one little problem," said Spike.

"And what's that?" replied Scorpion.

Spike tapped his watch with a twig.

"If we spend too much time hunting down these little robbers we're going to run out of time. We need to find a dragon's egg and then shoot one of the blasted things."

"Let me worry about that," said Scorpion. "You just do what you're told – when you're told to do it. Besides, this little job won't take very long."

He scowled, picked up his hunting knife, and viciously stabbed it into a stump.

"Hurry up with breakfast, you lazy fools. We need to get moving."

Paddy and Flynn watched the men as they silently gulped down their porridge.

"What do we do now?" whispered Paddy. "We can't do anything against them. They have knives and guns, and they're much bigger than us. We should have told Mum and Dad."

"Shhh," whispered Flynn. "I need to think. Let's just watch them for a while."

The men packed up their camp. They stuffed their sleeping bags and cooking equipment into their backpacks, and strapped their knives to their belts. Scorpion pulled out a compass and stared at it for a while. Without warning, he suddenly looked up – directly towards where the boys were hiding!

"Get down!" hissed Paddy, and the brothers flattened themselves on the ground. Scorpion seemed to sense something was wrong. He looked in their direction for a long time, before returning his compass to his backpack. Finally, he pulled his phone from his pocket and checked it for any messages.

When Paddy saw the phone in Scorpion's hand, a plan began to form in his mind. He turned to Flynn.

"We have to split them up, and get that device somehow. Then we can figure out what's on the rest of these papers. It might be our only chance to stop them from carrying out their mission."

Flynn's eyes widened.

"So, you want them to go in separate directions, and then you're going to ask nice Mr Scorpion there if you can borrow his device. That's the craziest thing I ever heard."

Paddy smiled.

"Don't worry. I know just how to do it."

CHAPTER 12

An hour later, Scorpion called a halt. He needed a rest. He was furious, because for that whole hour they had been battling their way through the thick forest. He had fallen over vines, slipped on tree roots and been whipped in the face by branches.

Scar was complaining. "Enough of this! Let's just do the job we came here to do," he whinged.

Scorpion lashed out and thumped him on the ear.

"You'll do what I tell you to do. And what I'm telling you to do right now is find those kids!"

Just then, he heard a strange whistle from the forest. He looked up, and there, plain as day, stood a boy. He had a smile on his face, and an arrow notched in his bow. Without a word he let fly. The arrow neatly skewered Spike's black cap, whipping it off his head and sticking it to a tree behind him.

Then Scar suddenly let out a loud howl. Scorpion turned to see him jumping up and down and rubbing his bottom! Another boy, slightly older, was standing on the other side of them, a slingshot dangling from his hand.

Before Scorpion had time to react, the boys had melted away into the forest.

He leapt into action.

"You two go after the small one. The big one's mine!" he yelled, bolting after Flynn.

Spike and Scar took off in one direction, Scorpion the other. He ran hard – as fast as he could, but the boy was quick and nimble through the trees.

But he was gaining on him. In fact, he had almost caught him! Scorpion stretched out his hand to grab the boy by the collar, but he ducked at the last second and swerved away.

But now the track straightened, and Scorpion could see that there was no getting through the thick forest on each side. He was catching up on the boy very quickly. It would be no more than a few seconds before Scorpion could clean up this little problem and get on with The Pitbull's mission.

The boy leapt and turned like a gazelle in front of him, but it wasn't going to help him now.

Then, all of a sudden, Scorpion was upside down, and he hadn't the faintest idea how it had happened. One minute he was sprinting for all his worth along a forest track, and the next he was hanging by his ankles from a flax rope and a tall, bendy tree.

Scorpion realised he was caught in a trap. When he'd stepped inside it, he had triggered it, and the tree, which had been bent over, snapped back upright and tightened a flax noose around his ankles. It had flipped him upside down, and now he dangled helplessly from it.

Suddenly the boy was beside him, smiling mischievously. Scorpion thrashed his arms about, trying to grab a hold of him. Each time he did this, the boy nimbly stepped back and threw a loop of rope around each of Scorpion's hands, and within seconds he had lashed his arms to the sides of his body. Try as he might to reach his knife and cut himself free, he couldn't do it. The boy had tied the rope tightly, and he couldn't move a muscle.

"Let me go!" he bellowed. "I'll squash you like a cockroach! I'll crush your puny little skull! You'll pay for this… with your life!" he shouted.

The boy began to twist Scorpion around and around, winding up the rope. It wrapped tighter and tighter around his ankles.

"What do you think you're doing?!" he yelled. "Stop, or I'll pulverise you!"

Suddenly the smaller boy and a dog appeared out of the undergrowth. The boy ran straight over to help his brother. Enthusiastically, the two of them twisted Scorpion around and around. He bellowed at them to stop, but they ignored him.

"This is going to be fun," said the smaller boy.

"Did it all go to plan with the other two?" asked his brother.

"They'll be a while yet," replied the boy with a smile. "Is that enough, do you think?"

Scorpion looked nervously at his legs. "Enough for what?" he asked. "Let me go!"

"Give it a few more," said the older boy. They wound the cord up as tightly as it would go. It was starting to hurt Scorpion's ankles.

"That should do it," said the older boy. Stepping back, he deftly flicked Scorpion's phone out of his pocket and put it into his own.

"Give that back!" he cried.

Then, Scorpion began to unwind. Around and around he went, faster and faster. With each rotation he noticed the boys were a little further away, walking backwards with broad grins on their faces. But soon, the forest was little more than a blur.

He heard one say to the other: "Now?"

"Now."

As Scorpion spun at ever increasing speed, he thought he could see the younger boy lifting his bow and taking aim at him.

"Noooooo!" he shouted.

Then suddenly Scorpion was falling. With a sickening crunch, he crashed to the ground. The boy had shot his arrow, which sliced through the flax holding his ankles. Bellowing like a bull, Scorpion staggered to his feet and tried to chase the boys, but found he couldn't run straight. He was so dizzy he immediately swerved right off the track and ran straight into the trunk of a tree. He got back up, but fell over again just as quickly, this time skinning his shin on a root.

"Aaarrggh!" he yelled.

Finally Scorpion was able to stand. He wobbled slightly, searching the forest for the boys. There was no sign of them, and he had no idea in which direction they had gone.

He heard a noise behind him and turned to see Scar and Spike coming out of the undergrowth. They were empty handed.

"Where the heck were you?" he roared at them.

"Chasing the boy. Couldn't catch him," said Spike. "Every time we caught up to him he'd disappear again. I think he was playing with us. I even heard him singing at one point."

Scar piped up.

"I notice you're empty handed too," he said. "Now, can we please just get on with what we came here to do?"

Scorpion screamed with rage, smashing his boot into a tree trunk.

CHAPTER 13

"It's one thing being able to get away from those men like we did, but it's quite another forcing them to leave the island," said Flynn.

The two boys had stopped to rest, eat a snack, and take a drink of water.

"You're right. But that was a lot of fun," replied Paddy. "I say we do it again!"

"I think we might want to look at the rest of these pictures first, and find out exactly what they're planning," said Flynn. He pulled from his pockets the folded pages and Scorpion's device – the boys had heard the men calling it a 'phone'. It was exactly the same as the other one.

"Let me see that," said Paddy, and took the phone off Flynn. He pushed the button at the bottom and it lit up. "Good, it looks like this one might last a while. The little rectangle is almost full – see?"

All of a sudden, the phone in Paddy's hand began to vibrate and make a loud beeping noise. The boys had never heard anything like it in their lives. Coco growled and backed away. Paddy threw it to the ground in alarm. Flynn saw he was about to stomp on it and managed to grab him just in time.

"Wait! What did you do?" asked Flynn.

"Nothing! I swear," protested Paddy. "It just started buzzing all by itself."

The boys stood watching the phone, buzzing and beeping on the ground between them. Flynn was ready to either run away or smash it to pieces at the first sign of trouble. But it just lay there, buzzing and beeping. The brothers crept closer to look at the screen.

"There's a green arrow moving from one side to the other on the front of it," said Paddy. "I think it wants us to move our finger over it."

"I don't think we should touch…"

But it was too late. Paddy had swiped at the green arrow and the buzzing and beeping abruptly stopped.

"There. I've stopped it. What a relief!"

As silence once again descended upon the forest, Flynn now heard another noise… very faintly.

"Can you hear something else?" he asked, tilting his head to one side.

"I think so," said Paddy. "It sounds like when there's a mosquito in our bedroom at night."

Paddy moved closer to the phone and Flynn saw his eyes widen with surprise.

"It's coming from this! It sounds like someone speaking!"

The boys both immediately tried to get their ears as close as possible to the phone, banging their heads together in the process.

"Ouch," said Flynn. "Clumsy fool!"

"Speak for yourself," replied Paddy, rubbing his sore head.

More carefully this time, they brought their ears as close as possible to the phone on the ground. Sure enough, Flynn could make out the angry voice of a man.

"He doesn't sound very happy," he said.

"How is this even possible?" marvelled Paddy, picking up the phone. The boys stood side by side, with the phone sandwiched between their ears. Now they could both clearly hear what the man was saying.

"What have you done with my men?" the angry voice asked. "You pesky little runts! You meddling little trouble-makers! You despicable, horrible little rodents! If you have interfered with my men and their mission I'll have you thrown into my zoo! I'll have you thrashed with sticks! I'll crush you like insects! Hello? Hello? Is anybody there?"

To Flynn's amazement, he suddenly realised that the man must be talking to them!

"Hello?" said Paddy.

"Hello?" the voice replied.

"Hello?" said Paddy again. "Is anybody in there?"

"Yes! Hello! Hello!" yelled the man. "What's the matter with you?"

"Hello?" said Paddy.

"If I catch you I'm going to have you whipped!" said the man.

"That's not going to happen," said Flynn.

"How on earth did you get yourself in there?" asked Paddy. "Are you a tiny little person?"

"Am I a tiny little… what are you talking about? I'll have you flayed alive!" raged the man.

"What's your name?" asked Paddy. "Mine's Paddy. And this is my brother Flynn. Very pleased to meet you."

"My name? MY NAME!? MY NAME IS THE PITBULL! I'M THE SCARIEST MAN ON THE

PLANET! I'LL MAKE YOU WISH YOU'D NEVER HEARD MY NAME!" screamed the man.

"I know you," said Paddy. "You're the little man from the screen. What happened to your face? Maybe you should have a nice cup of warm milk and a cookie and try to calm yourself down," he suggested. "You seem upset."

The Pitbull went to a whole new level of anger. "I'LL BREAK YOUR BONES! WHERE ARE MY MEN?! WHAT HAVE YOU DONE WITH MY MEN?!"

Flynn smiled. "They're busy."

Added Paddy: "And dizzy." The boys giggled.

As The Pitbull continued to rant and rave, Paddy held up the phone to show Flynn. In the centre was a red button, which Paddy had guessed might stop the man from talking. Flynn nodded enthusiastically – the man was giving him a headache.

Once more Paddy spoke into the phone.

"It's been lovely talking to you. Goodbye."

"Goodbye," called Flynn.

Flynn could hear The Pitbull going absolutely bananas as Paddy tapped the red button on the phone, and once again it was nice and quiet.

"Ahh – peace," said Flynn.

"He definitely needs some warm milk," said Paddy.

"I agree," said Flynn. "Now, let's take another look at these papers.

"OK," said Paddy. "This one first." He smoothed out the picture of the eight arrows on a nearby log.

Paddy aimed the phone at it.

"Hold it steady," he said.

Use the **AR Reads** app on your device to see what The Pitbull has planned for his men, and exactly where they must go to carry out their mission. Point the device at this page and watch the map come alive! If you don't have a device – don't worry – just keep reading!

The boys gasped in surprise when they saw a map of their island come to life on the screen of the phone. The view was of the Eastern Bays and the black boat anchored in the cove. A dotted line then appeared, which travelled to the Mother's Knee Hill. Flynn's heart sank. The brothers had visited there once with their father and seen the dragons' eggs dotted all over the hillside. Every female dragon on the island journeyed there to lay her eggs – it was their hatchery. Then, before she left, each female would use her teeth to grind rocks into egg-shaped boulders which were placed on the hillside alongside the eggs where they acted as a decoy so that predators couldn't tell which was an egg and which was simply a rock. If a wolf bit into a rock by mistake it would soon give up trying.

An instruction came on screen – 'Find a dragon's egg. Prepare for air lift'. Again the dotted line moved – this time to a crater at the end of the Mystic Mountains.

It was labelled 'Dragon's Crater'. Another instruction appeared: 'Kill a dragon'. The boys looked at each other in amazement and horror.

When the dotted trail ended back in the Eastern Bays, and the boat departed, an aircraft suddenly flew onto the screen, giving Flynn a fright. He'd seen something like it before in books, and remembered it was called a helicopter. It picked up the egg, and the dead dragon, and disappeared.

"Of course they were going to try to steal the egg from the Mother's Knee Hill," exclaimed Paddy.

"And they know about Dragon's Crater – where the rest of the dragons live!" said Flynn urgently. "How did they find out?"

Paddy was grim. "Those planes were flying over the island for weeks. So, the question is – what do we do now?"

"We have to follow them and try to stop them."

"But how?" asked Paddy.

"I don't know. I'm hoping we can figure it out on the way."

"Do you think they might still be searching for us? Or maybe they're on their way to the Mother's Knee?"

"By the sound of things, I think they're on their way," said Flynn. He had heard a *'squee!'*, high in the sky. "Quick, let's hide and wait for them to pass by."

The boys scrambled up a ridge and lay down in the grass. From here they would see the men coming. But Coco heard them first. Her body stiffened. Her nose twitched and she let out a soft whine.

"I know, girl," said Paddy. "They smell terrible."

"Shhh," said Flynn, and flattened himself to the ground as he saw the three men emerge from the forest. They looked tired and angry and were covered in scratches and bruises.

"If only we had more time I'd track down those little rats and skin them alive," said Scorpion.

"I'd wring their scrawny little necks," agreed Scar.

"That would be the easy part," said Spike. "Catching them's the problem."

"I'm not going to bother trying to catch them next time," said Scorpion. "I'm just going to shoot them."

Hearing this, Flynn pressed himself even lower to the ground until the men had passed and were out of sight.

"We're going to have to be very careful," said Flynn. "If they see us following them, it'll be all over."

The boys set off after the men. They relied on Coco rather than keeping them in sight. The dog was easily able to follow them at a safe distance by sniffing out their trail. Lightning, realising that Coco had taken over the job of tracking the men, flew in to sit on Flynn's shoulder. He had been up in the air for a long time and needed a rest.

Within an hour they had moved to higher ground. They were entering the hilly part of the island, where the Mystic Mountains rose up into the clouds. Soon, across the treetops, they would see the crest of the

Mother's Knee Hill – and the dragon hatchery. Then it was just a matter of cutting through the Colossal Forest to get there.

Now that there were fewer trees, it was more difficult for the boys to stay out of sight. They dropped even further back, and ran from rock to rock, ducking behind them. Once Paddy even stumbled and fell. Hearing the noise, Scar turned quickly to investigate. Luckily, Flynn had acted fast, grabbing both his brother and Coco, and dragging them into a hollow in the ground.

"That was close," said Paddy. He closed his eyes. "Can't we just lie here and sleep for a while?"

"I'm afraid not," said his brother. "I'm tired too. Let's have something to eat."

But the boys only had some bread crusts and half a dozen squishy apricots left in their rucksacks. They gave the bread to Coco, and ate the apricots all at once, knowing that if they really had to they could find wild food from the forest.

"Come on," said Flynn. "I'm pretty sure Mother's Knee Hill isn't far now."

Sure enough, ten minutes later they reached a ridge top from which they could see the oddly shaped hill. It was speckled with oval eggs and rocks, and just as he remembered, Flynn couldn't tell one from the other.

The boys could see the three men on the hillside. They had split up and were examining each rock in case it might be a dragon's egg.

"I think we might be here for a while," said Paddy. "Hey, we didn't get time to look at that last picture before that lot turned up."

"You're right," said Flynn. "Let's do it now."

Flynn pulled the phone and the piece of paper from his pocket.

"Oh no. I've torn it," he said, unfolding it gently.

A rip went right through the picture of the egg with the dragon curled up inside it.

Paddy pushed the button to start up the phone.

"Let's try it anyway. You hold the pieces together."

The boys tried for ten minutes, but the rip had ruined it. No matter how they tried, nothing showed on the screen.

"It's no good. It won't work," said Paddy, screwing up the paper and flinging it away in disgust.

Flynn had been holding the phone in one hand and the paper in the other when Paddy ripped it away.

"Hey," he complained, but then fell silent. Something was happening. Now that the paper had gone, the phone was pointed directly at the Mother's Knee Hill.

This is the Mother's Knee Hill. Use the **AR Reads** app on your device to see how the men find out which of the oval-shaped objects on the hill is a real dragon's egg, and which is only a rock, cleverly carved by dragons. Point the device at this page and see for yourself! If you don't have a device, don't worry – just keep reading!

Paddy came to look at the screen.

"This shows exactly which ones are eggs!" he exclaimed. "Look, the eggs are glowing blue, while the rocks stay grey. This must be how the men figure out which is which."

"Except now they can't tell, because we have this," said Flynn, holding up the phone.

"They must be so mad with us," said Paddy with a cheeky smile.

Flynn looked across at the hill. The men were moving from rock to rock, putting their ear to each egg and tapping on it with a hammer. After an hour, Scorpion shouted in triumph and Scar and Spike ran over to join him. The three men gathered around the rock and examined it closely.

"See if he's found an egg," said Paddy.

Flynn held up the phone and pointed it at the hill. To his dismay, he saw the rock was glowing blue.

"It's an egg," he said.

"Oh no," replied Paddy. He thumped his fist into the ground.

The men, too, had realised they'd found one. They went right to work tying canvas straps around it, making a kind of harness so that a helicopter could pick it up and fly away with it. Within ten minutes, the job was done, and the egg was bound up tightly. Scorpion checked that the straps were secure and looked at his watch. He barked a command that Flynn couldn't hear, and the three men walked down off the hill into the Colossal Forest. They were heading in the direction of the crater on the Mystic Mountain range, where they knew the dragons lived.

"I think I know what to do," said Flynn. "But we haven't got much time."

CHAPTER 14

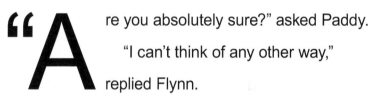re you absolutely sure?" asked Paddy.

"I can't think of any other way," replied Flynn.

Paddy whistled. The plan that his brother had just explained to him was breathtakingly dangerous.

"OK. Let's do it," he said.

Flynn pulled out the piece of paper with the compass points on it.

"We won't be needing this again," he said. Turning it over, he wrote on the back.

Dear Mum, Dad, Grandma, and Grandad,

If you're reading this note, Lightning did his job and delivered it to you.

We don't have time to explain what's going on right now, but you need to do exactly as we say – please. You need to trust us – it's a matter of life and death!

You need to send Lightning back to Paddy, right away, but you also need to make sure Clappers follows him. Give her a smack on the rump so that she knows she has to run as fast as possible.

Granny, this is going to sound strange, but you need to sail your yacht to the Eastern Bays of The Island. Bring Dad with you. Once there, you'll see a black boat – it is anchored in the bay, with a dinghy on the shore.

Take the black boat back out through the Gulp Swallow Pass (towing the dinghy) and anchor it offshore – outside the reef. Then use the dinghy to get back into the bay to your yacht.

Wait for us there, and be ready to go.

Mum, you stay at home with Grandad and Ada.

Please don't come looking for us. We can't tell you why, but you must do as we say.

We love you.

Flynn and Paddy

Flynn rolled up the note and tied it to Lightning's leg with a leather string. "Home, Lightning, as fast as you can!" he said. He patted the bird on the head, and then flung him into the air. The falcon spread his wings, and within seconds he was gone, speeding like an arrow towards their home.

Flynn turned to his brother.

"Time to go," he said.

Paddy looked at him.

"You sure you don't want to swap missions?"

He smiled, but inside his stomach was in knots.

"Go. Quickly!" Flynn gave Paddy a hug. "Please be careful."

"You too," replied Paddy. Then he was gone, Coco at his heels, running like the wind along the ridge before disappearing into the forest.

CHAPTER 15

Flynn's fingers shook as he struggled to release the clips. The men had bound the dragon's egg so tightly it was difficult to undo. It was a good ten minutes before he had succeeded in taking all the straps off the egg. He had to stay alert in case any of the men returned. He must be ready to run away at any moment. At one point, he heard a noise and dived for cover behind a rock, before realising that it was just the bleating of a wild goat.

"Now to make sure they get themselves a nice fat rock," he said to himself with a grin. He walked fifty steps back from the hill, pulled out the phone, and aimed it at the slope. As before, the eggs glowed blue, while the rocks remained grey. Using the phone, Flynn selected a nice big rock close to where the men had trussed up the egg.

Working quickly, Flynn dragged all the straps to the big rock. He tied the straps to it, trying to make it look like the men had done it.

It was another ten minutes before he was satisfied, and he sat back to examine his work. It was trussed up nicely, with a steel clip at the top where a helicopter could attach a hook.

"I hope this works," he said to himself.

Picking up his rucksack and slingshot, Flynn plunged back into the forest and ran towards the Mystic Mountains. He ran until his lungs were fit to burst, and even then he didn't slow down. He was afraid he had spent too much time strapping up the rock, and feared he might be too late to stop the men from killing a dragon.

The other problem was that he only roughly knew where he was going. He must be careful he didn't suddenly come upon the men.

Flynn ran out of the Colossal Forest and up into the mountains. He kept running until he could see that he was approaching a large basin – the crater of an ancient volcano.

When Flynn got near the edge of the crater, he slowed to a walk. Finally, he stopped and lay down on his stomach. Keeping as low as he could, he dragged himself to the lip of the crater. As he came to the edge, he suddenly heard voices. At the same time he saw something so incredible, it took his breath away.

CHAPTER 16

Paddy was exhausted. He could barely see straight, but he kept running. He didn't know how far he had travelled and he wasn't sure how much longer he could keep it up. He was discovering just what his body was capable of.

Paddy was concentrating so hard on trying not to trip as he ran that he almost crashed into Clappers.

The horse was running hard in the opposite direction, following Lightning's cries from high above. Her hooves skidded in the leaves as she came to a stop.

"Clappers!" yelled Paddy. "Am I glad to see you!" He threw his arms around her neck as she whinnied softly.

Just then, Lightning came swooping silently through the trees, turned sharply, and landed on Paddy's shoulder.

"Good boy, Lightning," said Paddy. He could see there was a note attached to the falcon's leg. He untied the string, unrolled the note and recognised his mother's handwriting.

Dear boys,

We are so very worried, but we have done just as you asked. Please be careful and hurry home to us.

Love, Mum, Dad, Granny, Grandad, and Ada.

Clappers pawed the ground, then lowered her head to nuzzle Paddy's face. Paddy laughed and whispered in her ear.

"You're going to have to run like crazy, Clappers. Faster than you've ever run before. Are you ready?"

Clappers let out a loud neigh. She was ready.

Paddy leapt upon her back, glad to finally give his tired legs a rest. He gripped the horse's body with his knees, and held tight to her powerful neck.

"Let's go," he shouted, turning his horse in the direction of Mt Monstrous.

CHAPTER 17

I n every direction Flynn looked, there was a flying dragon. If he'd been able to stop the whirling, swooping dragons for a moment, he guessed he would have counted over a hundred of them, soaring in the sky, or zooming low over the bottom of the crater. It was truly an incredible sight.

He and Paddy had never been allowed here before. For a minute he simply watched, his mouth hanging open at the spectacle. He marvelled at the way they flew – able to turn almost as quickly as a swallow and fly almost as fast as a falcon.

They twisted and soared upside down, or looped the loop with ease.

There was an incredible array of colours. Some were sky blue. Others were the deep green of the sea on a cloudy day. Flynn saw two dragons that were fiery orange, and yet another as yellow as a canary. There were pinks, blues, and reds of every description. Some of the dragons were even a snowy white. All of them had a sparkling, shimmering quality to their skin – like that of a fish, or a snake.

Every so often one of the dragons would breathe out a powerful and terrifically hot streak of fire. Indeed, there wasn't a green tree or bush to be seen in the entire crater; everything had been burned black by the dragons' fire.

Suddenly, Flynn heard the sound of the men's voices again, coming from somewhere below him on the slope of the crater. But he couldn't see anything. For a minute or two he watched carefully. Then a movement caught his eye.

The men were lying on a rock ledge under a blanket. The clever pattern on the blanket made it look the same colour as the ground. Flynn guessed that it was so the dragons wouldn't spot the men and attack them.

Then Flynn saw something that made his heart sink. The ugly black barrel of a large rifle protruded from under the blanket. The men were planning to shoot the first dragon that came close enough.

Flynn had to do something, and quickly!

Desperate for an idea, he looked around him. Nothing. Just a bunch of rocks scattered around the rim of the crater. They wouldn't be of much use against a gun.

Then, suddenly, it came to him.

He had a plan.

CHAPTER 18

Paddy couldn't quite believe what he was about to do.

Not only had he promised his parents, but he had vowed never again to venture near the top of Mt Monstrous. He was frightened for his life. It was a scary place – rocky and steep, with plunging cliffs down three sides. There were the blackened remains of tree stumps everywhere – burned by scorching fire.

Paddy shivered. This high up it was cold and windy. A freezing mist hung around the mountaintop.

He was looking for the dark opening of Big Red's cave, but he wasn't at all sure where it was.

Suddenly, as Paddy rounded a steep rock face, he saw it; its dark opening sent a chill through him. And there, protruding out of it a long way, was the dragon's thick and powerful tail.

He was frozen with fear, rooted to the spot. He felt as though all power had drained from his body. But he forced himself forward.

CHAPTER 19

Working quickly, Flynn dragged a dozen rocks to the very edge of the crater. He was directly up the slope from where the men were lying under their camouflaged blanket.

He placed the rocks carefully, in a pyramid-shaped stack, using a short, strong stick to prop up the rock at the very bottom of the pile.

Suddenly, there was a loud explosion. The men had fired the gun at a dragon! Flynn dived to the ground, hiding behind his rock pile. From his vantage point, he could see that the men had missed the dragon, but now, he expected a hundred dragons to launch an attack.

But, because of all the noise coming from the roaring dragons and their fiery breath, the sound of the gun went unnoticed – even by the lucky dragon that had almost lost its life.

Flynn knew he had to move quickly. Reaching into the leather pouch on his belt, he grabbed three stones, and put them into his mouth.

Staying on his belly, he pulled himself over the rim of the crater and started to slide down towards the men. As he slid, some small pebbles rolled down the hill. For a moment, Flynn froze as a shower of gravel travelled down the slope and pitter-pattered on the men's blanket. But the men were too absorbed in their work. They were trying to line up another dragon in the awful gun's sights.

Flynn was making for a rocky outcrop that lay just to one side of where the men were lying.

He judged it would be just large enough for him to hide behind.

Within thirty seconds, he was crouched behind it. Now he was close enough to hear what the men were saying.

"There's one circling, just there. It's coming closer. It's a beauty. Get ready – take aim," said Scorpion.

Flynn turned to look at the men's target. He gasped. It was a stunningly beautiful, bright green dragon with shimmering orange wings. Its skin seemed to glow and pulse as the light reflected from its scales. He was spellbound by the amazing way it flew – making tiny adjustments to its wings to fly and turn with incredible speed, power, and grace. He knew in that moment that he would do anything to stop it from being killed.

Flynn looked up at his rock pile. The time was now. He knew he would have just one chance.

CHAPTER 20

Halfway across The Island, Paddy fought to keep his nerves under control. His hands shook and his legs felt like they might give way beneath him.

Drawing back his bow, Paddy aimed for the very end of Big Red's tail.

With a deep breath he steadied himself and let fly. He was dead on target.

There came a roar so terrifically loud that it shook the earth.

CHAPTER 21

In one smooth movement, Flynn took a stone from his mouth and placed it in the pocket of his slingshot. He pulled it back to his cheek. There was no time for taking careful aim; he would have to shoot through pure instinct. Without hesitation, he let loose the best shot he had ever taken.

The stone flew with pinpoint accuracy at the rock pile. But not just at the rock pile; in fact, the

stone was speeding towards the short, stout stick that held the rock pile in place. It struck it perfectly in the centre, snapping it clean in two.

Flynn held his breath. One by one, the rocks tumbled down the hill, straight towards the men.

CHAPTER 22

Paddy slid and sprinted down through the sparse forest and rocky slopes of Mt Monstrous, faster than he had ever run before. He had already cut his shin badly on a sharp piece of rock, and his face was bleeding from the thorns of an overhanging blackberry bush. But it didn't slow him down at all. He ran so quickly and on such a steep slope that he almost fell several times. As he passed by small trees, he grabbed them to steady himself.

Paddy didn't dare take even one look behind him. He could hear the terrific noise of trees being toppled like matchsticks, giant rocks being dislodged and rolling down the hill, and worst of all, the dragon's terrible roars.

Despite how quickly Paddy was running, he knew Big Red was catching up. But he was close to the bottom of Mount Monstrous and the relative safety of the thicker forest. There the dragon would have trouble spotting him. He might just make it in time!

When Paddy suddenly came to the edge of a cliff, he realised in horror that he had taken a wrong turn. It wasn't a high cliff, but it was far too high to jump down without breaking an ankle. At the bottom of it he could see Coco, who had run off ahead at the sound of the dragon's roar, and Clappers, who had been happily chewing on new fern fronds, but now stood to attention as she heard the terrible sound of the dragon coming down the hill.

There was no time to retrace his steps and come down safely. Paddy was trapped! He looked up the hill to see Big Red smash through the last line of trees as if they were made of paper. Paddy saw a huge ball of fire forming in the back of his open mouth.

Desperately, he looked around him. Then, he saw his only chance. A young tree grew at the very edge of the cliff. Its trunk was no thicker than Paddy's wrist, but it was tall and strong. Somehow it had managed to grow amongst the rocks, its roots snaking around them and down into the soil.

Paddy ran to it, and leaping up, grabbed the tree as high up the trunk as he could. As he'd hoped, it bent over like a fishing rod under his weight. He climbed the trunk higher and it bent some more. He expected it to snap at any moment, but it held. As he moved along the trunk, it bent more and more, until slowly he sank below the top of the cliff.

Suddenly, above him, Paddy felt a ferocious heat as Big Red's fireball flew across the ground and out over the edge of the cliff. Clappers gave a loud, frightened whinny from below, but bravely she held her ground.

The fireball set the stump of the small tree ablaze and weakened it. Paddy began to drop even further towards the ground. He swung his legs. Just as the tree cracked and broke, Paddy let go, flying through the air and landing squarely on Clappers' back. She reared up on her hind legs.

"Ruuuuuunnnnnn!" he yelled, and the horse took off so fast that Paddy could barely hold on. At breakneck speed, Clappers leaped over large boulders and fallen trees.

Paddy turned to look. To his horror, Big Red had taken to the air and was swooping down on them with such velocity it made his hair stand on end.

Just ahead, Paddy could see the forest! But, just before it, there was a decent-sized, fast-flowing river that had been tricky to cross on the way up.

This time Clappers did not mean to wade carefully across the river. She gained even more speed, and Paddy could not have controlled her even if he'd wanted to.

As Paddy realised that Clappers was going to jump, he saw Coco out of the corner of his eye, a brown blur streaking along beside them. She was running at the speed of a lioness, her back arching and bending with the effort. But she would never make it across the river in time to get away from Big Red and there was no way she could leap across it!

"Coco!" he yelled. "Up! Up!"

Coco understood. Making use of a fallen tree that sloped gently upwards, she ran along the trunk and leapt into Paddy's outstretched arms.

At the same time Paddy felt the horse's muscles bunch and coil up underneath him as she prepared to make the biggest jump of her life.

She leaped. Her nose stretched forward, her ears flattened against the top of her head. Her front legs curled up high under her chest, and her back legs and tail streamed out behind her. For the longest time she seemed to hang in the air, and Paddy felt like he was flying.

An incredible roar came from right behind them, but Clappers didn't miss a beat. She landed on the other side of the river without breaking her stride. Paddy, off balance due to the weight of his heavy dog, almost fell, but managed to grip Clappers' body with his knees. In seconds Clappers, Coco and Paddy had raced headlong into the thick forest.

CHAPTER 23

At the same moment Scar pulled the trigger, he was struck on the back of the neck by the first of the rocks. The gun fired, but his aim was off because of the falling rock, and the bullet missed the green dragon by inches.

Flynn saw the dragon shudder in the air. He saw its head swivel towards the men. In the same instant, Flynn realised that the dragon had also spotted him.

The rest of the rocks bounced down the hill, most of them harmlessly missing the men. Flynn knew that they weren't big enough to really hurt them, but that was also part of his plan.

The men threw back the blanket, and shouting in anger, looked up the hill from where the rocks had come. They ran to find the culprit.

Flynn saw his chance as the men scrambled up the hill. Keeping low, he sprinted across to the rock shelf on which the men had been lying and dived down below it. He reached up over the ledge and his fingers searched out the cold steel of the rifle's barrel.

Flynn took the two remaining stones from his mouth and pushed them as deep as he could into the barrel of the gun.

Now he had to get out of sight. But, just as he was about to scramble back to the cover of his rock, he heard the men's voices above him on the ledge. They had come back to finish the job!

"Am I bleeding?" Scar said. "I've got a terrible headache."

"Hush up!" snapped Scorpion. "Stop crying and shoot one of the stupid things."

Flynn flattened himself to the ground. He was directly below them, and only just out of sight. When he looked up he could see the barrel of the gun moving onto its target.

Suddenly, from behind him, came a terrific roar. Without turning around, he knew that it was the green dragon. His heart sank.

"Now!" shouted Scorpion. "FIRE!"

There was a blinding flash and a deafening explosion.

Dazed, shocked, and unbearably sad, Flynn dropped his head into the dirt.

CHAPTER 24

Paddy rode Clappers with all his skill as she zig-zagged her way through the trees at top speed. Sometimes he had to slide over to the side of her body and hold on tightly to her neck as she ran under low branches. Coco galloped alongside, happy to be off the back of the horse.

All the while, above them, Paddy could see Big Red flying above the treetops, but the dragon could do little to catch them and had to be content with roaring loudly. Once he swooped and sent a scorching fireball down towards them as they crossed another stream, but they were gone into the forest on the other side before it hit the ground.

But Paddy could see that this time Big Red wasn't going to simply give up – he was intent on revenge.

Every now and again Paddy heard a *'squee'*, and knew that Lightning was sounding the alarm that the dragon was getting close. In this way, he and Clappers moved safely through the forest.

CHAPTER 25

When Scar fired the gun, there was a blinding flash and a *boom* so loud it almost burst Scorpion's eardrums. He saw the recoil from the rifle smash the butt so hard into Scar's shoulder that the idiot almost lost his grip on the gun.

When the smoke cleared, Scorpion looked at the barrel in disbelief. It had split open and peeled back like a banana skin. It was completely ruined. Slowly he regained his senses. He'd read about this sort of thing – it usually happened when the barrel was blocked – often if it has been dropped into the mud and stones had become lodged in the barrel.

But the men had been so careful not to let anything like that happen – he'd personally cleaned and oiled himself that morning. It was as clean as a whistle.

He stared hard at Scar. The fool must have dropped the gun when he wasn't watching. He balled his hand into a fist.

But just then, the older of the two boys stood up right in front of them, opened his mouth wide, and roared like a wild animal!

Scorpion recoiled, jumping to his feet. He promptly fell backwards over Spike. Scar let out a high-pitched squeal. Scorpion got back up, but became entangled in the camouflage blanket and went down again.

The boy bolted. He ran up the hill, over the edge of the crater and disappeared from view. By the time Scorpion and the other two had disentangled themselves and run up to the crater's rim, the little rat was almost at the trees.

As Scorpion watched, he saw the boy stop, turn and search the sky above them. Scorpion got a prickling sensation of fear, and followed the boy's gaze, directly above him. There, plummeting from the sky like a giant bird of prey, was the green dragon, a fireball growing in its mouth.

Scorpion said nothing. He simply put his head down and ran for his life towards the forest, after the boy who had now disappeared among the trees. Scar and Spike raced after him, just making it to the safety of the trees before the green dragon swooped down and set the grass ablaze with a hot streak of fire.

CHAPTER 26

A *'squee!'* above him let Paddy know to be on the lookout for something up ahead. He hoped like mad it was his brother, alive and well, rather than anything or anyone else. He couldn't bring himself to think about what might happen if either of them failed in their missions.

Clappers was breathing hard. Paddy had pushed her harder than he ever had before, but she hadn't slowed down one bit. She still galloped through the forest at a tremendous pace, with Coco hard at her heels.

The horse heard Lightning's call, too, so when she rounded a tree and saw Flynn, running for his life through the forest towards them, she let out a loud whinny of greeting.

Flynn looked pleased to see them – he was obviously worn out. As Flynn and the horse converged onto the same path, Paddy leaned over towards his brother. He made a hoop with his elbow. Flynn put out his arm and caught Paddy's, swinging himself around and up onto the back of their horse in one flowing movement. It was a trick the boys had practiced many times before.

Paddy heard the men give a frustrated cry behind them. They were clearly upset to see that they were now trying to catch up with a horse.

"You took ages," said Paddy. "Did it all go to plan?"

"More or less," replied Flynn. "How about you?"

The sound of Big Red's flapping wings came from above.

"Can you hear him up there?" asked Paddy. "He's mighty grumpy."

"Good job," said Flynn, smiling.

"Now what?" asked Paddy.

"Now we let Big Red teach these men some manners," said Flynn.

"I like the sound of that," replied Paddy.

"I stopped them from shooting a dragon," said Flynn. It was obvious he couldn't wait to tell his brother all about it.

"Of course you did," said Paddy. "I'd expect nothing less."

"You should see the one they were trying to shoot, Paddy. He's… incredible. He's huge and graceful and so fast and strong. He's beautiful – as green as an emerald, with wings the colour of the sunset."

"Phew," said Paddy. "I'd like to see that."

"It's not over yet," said Flynn. "Slow down a bit. We need to let those men catch up."

Paddy leaned back and Clappers responded, slowing to a walk. He listened as Flynn told him the plan.

The trees thinned out as they made their towards the Eastern Bays. They were making for a large clearing in the forest in which the boys sometimes stopped to rest when they were out exploring. Paddy kept Clappers at a steady pace, and the men doggedly followed them.

Paddy also kept a close eye on Big Red.

When they reached the edge of the clearing, they stopped. Paddy turned the horse around. Above them, Big Red silently circled, high above. The whole way through the forest, he hadn't made a sound.

The men stumbled out of the trees, obviously tired and worn out. Seeing the boys sitting quietly on Clappers' back, they pulled up, clearly surprised to have caught up with them. An ugly smile spread across Scorpion's face as he drew his long knife. In response Coco growled and bared her teeth.

"This is your last chance," said Flynn. "You need to leave this island, and never come back."

Scar and Spike nodded in agreement, but Scorpion simply clenched his teeth and raised his knife. He was shaking with rage.

"And you can tell your boss to give up trying to kill or own a dragon," added Paddy. "They're supposed to be free – not in some zoo, or stuffed and put on display."

"You little rats!" yelled Scorpion. "You'll be sorry!" He walked towards the boys. Scar and Spike, obviously realising their choice had been made for them, followed close behind.

Flynn shrugged.

"Suit yourself," he said.

Paddy spun Clappers around to face the open clearing.

He waited until the men were almost upon them, then whispered into Clappers' ear.

"Giddy-up!"

Clappers took off across the clearing like a cheetah. The men broke into a run after them.

Above, Big Red turned and swooped.

The men had no idea that the world's most ferocious dragon was in a high-speed dive of death right above them. They chased the boys and their horse out into the middle of the clearing.

Clappers rocketed across the open space. Paddy swivelled, and looked up into the sky. The dragon was bearing down on them, but it was clear that the horse was too fast. The men, however, had barely made it to the centre of the clearing. As Paddy watched, he saw the dragon change course. Big Red was no longer heading for them, but instead had set his sights on the three hapless men.

Suddenly the dragon let forth a screaming roar that was so loud and terrifying the men froze in their tracks. Scorpion looked up in horror. Scar tripped and fell to the ground and lay there shaking like a leaf.

Spike dropped to his knees and appeared to be saying his prayers.

It would be all over in a matter of seconds.

CHAPTER 27

Having reached the safety of the trees, Flynn and Paddy leapt off their horse and turned to see the terrifying sight of Big Red bearing down on the three men.

"I think we might have to save them," said Paddy.

"Agreed," replied Flynn. Paddy dug his heels into Clappers' flanks, wheeling her back towards the centre of the clearing. Paddy yelled at Big Red. Flynn whistled loudly and waved his hands above his head.

It was enough to attract the attention of the dragon. He took one look at the brothers and changed course again. Now Big Red was coming for them, a fireball forming in his mouth.

Flynn's whistle, meanwhile, had been heard by Lightning, who true to his name, came hurtling down out of the sky like a bolt from a storm.

Flynn watched as Lightning folded his wings against his body and dropped like a stone, straight towards the red dragon's head. The beast was completely unaware that this tiny, fierce bundle of

feathers, beak and talons was about to properly introduce himself.

Just as Big Red ignited the ball of gas in his throat, Lightning was upon him, landing on his snout and pecking wildly at his eyes.

As well as enraging the dragon, it also put him off target, and his fireball hit the earth halfway between the boys and the three men. Flames spread across the clearing. Big Red screamed, twisting and turning, but was unable to rid himself of the brave bird.

The boys seized their chance.

The men had completely given up hope, so the brothers had to gallop right out to them to get their attention.

"This way!" yelled Paddy. "Now, or you'll be killed!"

The three men looked up at the boys with amazement. Although terrified, they seemed to understand that the brothers were trying to save them.

Paddy slid off Clappers' back and gave Scorpion a kick up the backside.

"RUUNNNN!" he yelled.

The men finally sprang into action. They got to their feet and ran for their lives. Paddy followed.

Sliding forward, Flynn dug a knee into Clappers' neck and wheeled her around. She took off, sprinting for the safety of the forest. Paddy was just ahead of them. Flynn leaned over and slid an arm under Paddy's, hoping to slingshot him around onto the back of the horse. But he misjudged, and Paddy glanced off Clappers' shoulder, sending him sprawling on the ground.

"Paddy!" yelled Flynn, wheeling Clappers around again. He would not leave his brother out here. He dug his heels hard into Clappers flanks.

But he knew he was too late. Big Red was upon them, blocking out the sun with his enormous bulk, his massive talons outstretched before him. Flynn braced for the impact.

A green streak slashed through the sky. There came the sound of a massive impact, or rather the feel of one, as the green dragon – the one from the crater – came out of nowhere, slamming into the side of Big Red at scarcely believable speed. It seemed to shake the very air. The red dragon was taken out of the sky and smashed into the earth, sent tumbling over and over right across the clearing, finally coming to rest against the tree trunks around the edge.

It took Flynn a moment to register what had just happened. He leapt down off the horse and pulled his brother to his feet, and the two of them stood there, staring across the clearing at the dragons. Big Red was dazed, and lay on his side. The green dragon stood, shook itself and then leapt into the air, flapping hard to rise out of the clearing. It circled them twice, looking down at the brothers, before it let forth a deafening roar, turned and flew away across the forest.

Flynn looked at Paddy. His brother was speechless, his face lit up with excitement.

"That was the green dragon you saved wasn't it?"

Flynn nodded.

"He repaid the favour," he said, shaking his head in disbelief.

As Flynn expected, the experience of almost being killed by Big Red had frightened the men so much that they weren't interested in fighting any more.

They lay among the trees, gasping with exhaustion and fright. Meanwhile, Big Red had recovered and taken to the air again. Every time they heard the red dragon roar, or his shadow fell over the forest, they twitched and whimpered in fright.

"Get up. Time to go," said Paddy.

Paddy had an arrow notched on his bow and Flynn had a stone in the leather pocket of his slingshot. Coco growled softly.

"You have two choices," said Flynn. "Either we leave you here, right now, and you figure out how to get home on your own; or, come with us, do exactly as we say, and you might stand a chance of escaping this island with your lives."

Spike nodded furiously, hoping that his leader would agree.

"Keep in mind that Big Red up there knows that you're weak. He will keep hunting you until he catches you," added Paddy.

Scar looked as though he might cry at any moment.

"So, what's it going to be?" asked Flynn.

"All right," said Scorpion. "You win."

"That's the first smart thing you've said since you got here," said Paddy with a smile.

CHAPTER 28

The sky was darkening when they finally reached the Eastern Bays. A bright orange glow showed where the sun had gone down in the west.

Paddy was tired beyond measure – it had not been easy giving Big Red the slip.

First, the brothers had kissed Clappers and Coco on their hairy noses and sent them home. The boys attached a note to Coco's collar, telling their mum not to worry.

Then came the job of hiding from Big Red as they made their way through the forest. Had it just been the brothers, it would have been easy. But the men were clumsy and so tired that they kept falling over logs and yelling out in pain. Each time Big Red heard the commotion and figured out where they were, they'd have to start the deadly game of hide and seek all over again.

The boys cut ferns and branches and attached them to the rucksacks and hats of the men to camouflage them. It worked. As evening fell and the gloom deepened, eventually Big Red lost sight of them.

Clearly angry at having to go hungry, the Red Dragon let forth a roar so loud that it made the three men shiver in fear. Then he turned for Mt Monstrous and flew away.

The coast was now clear, and the party were finally able to make their way back to the Eastern Bays.

Lightning fluttered down out of the trees and was sound asleep on Paddy's shoulder when the Bays finally came into view.

Paddy's heart leapt when he saw that instead of the black boat his grandparents' yacht was anchored in the cove. The black boat was just a tiny dark spot on the horizon, anchored well outside of the reef.

Paddy could see that it was a terrible shock to his father to see his two sons stumble out onto the beach with three large men as their prisoners. But he didn't let on to the men.

"Good evening, boys," he said brightly. "Everything's ready for you – just as you asked. Your grandmother's waiting on the yacht."

He pulled the dinghy down to the water's edge and held it steady. The three men made to get in.

"Not you," said their father sternly. "You can swim."

The long swim to the yacht took the last bit of energy from the men. When they finally dragged themselves up the ladder to the back of the yacht, they were no match for the boys' fierce little grandmother.

"If you think my grandsons are tough, then just wait and see what happens if you make me cross," she told them. "Now get yourselves up the front, and stay there until I tell you!" she ordered.

The men didn't protest. They walked up to the bow of the yacht and collapsed, completely exhausted.

When the boys came aboard their grandmother gave them a cuddle.

"You look like you've had a long day," she said. "Now, let's send these men home, shall we?"

As always, Paddy marvelled at his grandmother's ability to weave her way through the complicated reef. There wasn't so much as a scrape on the yacht's hull, and all done in near darkness. In ten minutes, they were out past the reef and bobbing up and down in a strong swell and a freshening wind – the beginnings of an ocean storm.

When they neared the black boat, their grandmother winked at the brothers, then looked sternly at the men.

"Over the side you go!" she yelled.

They protested.

"Please bring us a little closer," pleaded Spike.

"Flynn? Paddy?" said their grandmother.

The boys reached for their weapons; Paddy notched an arrow, and Flynn drew back a stone.

"Aim for their butts, boys!" yelled their grandmother.

With a frightened shout, the three men leapt off the yacht and swam like crazy for their boat.

"Watch out for the sharks!" called their father, which made the men howl and swim even faster.

CHAPTER 29

I t was late when the little yacht finally nosed into Home Lagoon. The boys were sound asleep under the starry sky, curled up on deck, and wrapped in the yacht's silky spinnaker. They didn't wake when their father carried them up to the house and laid them into their beds, nor when their mother kissed them, nor when their grandfather stroked their faces. They didn't even stir, when in the middle of the night, the full fury of the storm hit, lashing rain hard against the windows.

They slept the deepest sleep of their young lives. Very early the next morning, the three men were still only halfway home, battling large waves, soaked to the skin and so cold and tired they could hardly stand.

"I'm never going back to that island, long as I live," said Scar.

"Me neither," said Spike.

"Luckily we didn't completely fail," said Scorpion. "At least The Pitbull will get his dragon's egg."

Back on the island, Flynn and Paddy were woken by the thudding sound from the rotor blades of a helicopter passing over the house.

"That must be the helicopter," said Flynn. "It's a long way to come for a rock."

Paddy giggled. Then the dragon brothers turned over and fell back to sleep.

If you enjoyed reading The Dragon Defenders,
I'd be so grateful if you'd take the time to rate it
or write a review on Amazon.com

Thanks,

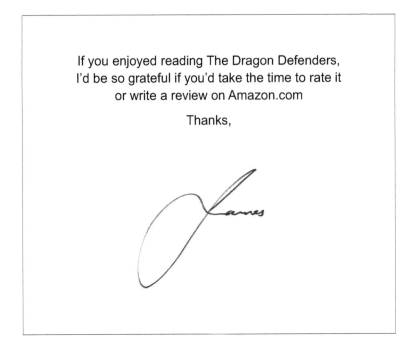

Get your FREE copy of The First Defender!

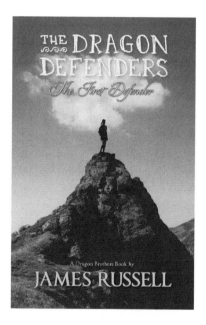

Have you ever wondered what living on a paradise island would be like?

The First Defender – a short novel which you can download for free – includes one of the stories from the diary of Flynn and Paddy's mother. Long before they were born, when she was just a girl – and the only child on The Island – she had some pretty thrilling adventures of her own.
You might even call her the original 'Dragon Defender'.

To get your free copy, visit
dl.bookfunnel.com/i12zk78xaa

Enjoyed The Dragon Defenders?

Here's chapter one of The Dragon Defenders
- Book Two: The Pitbull Returns...

CHAPTER 1

The Pitbull's jaw muscles bunched and bulged as he chewed his breakfast.

"Delicious," he declared, taking up his napkin and carefully wiping the corners of his mouth. "I think I'll have them again tomorrow."

He had just finished eating a dozen tiny blue-green eggs, which had been stolen the day before from the nest of a very rare species of sea turtle in Guatemala. He'd instructed his chef to boil them for exactly two minutes. They were served with two slices of cold toast spread with French foie gras –

the mashed up liver of a goose. The meal cost an absolute fortune. Dining on the turtle's eggs brought that species one step closer to extinction, but it didn't

worry The Pitbull one bit – in fact, it made him feel important.

"Are you going to eat those?" said The Pitbull, looking up.

The Pitbull sat at one end of a long, black marble dining table. It was decorated in the centre with the head of a snarling dog, inlaid into the glossy surface in white stone. A shimmering array of fine silverware and Egyptian cotton napkins surrounded him. Fresh flowers bloomed from a vase and today's newspaper lay neatly folded to one side. Behind him, a floor-to-ceiling window gave an astonishing view of the city. The Pitbull's dining room and office were forty floors up.

The Pitbull's niece, Briar, sat at the far end of the table. She was staring down at her own plate of turtle's eggs, a look of disgust on her face.

"No," she replied, "I'd rather starve."

"They're very healthy – I think," he insisted.

Briar said nothing.

The Pitbull smiled. Sooner or later she would figure out what was good for her.

"How old are you?" he asked. "Nine? Ten?"

"Eleven," replied Briar.

"Whatever. In any case, it's time you grew up,"
said The Pitbull. "Your parents are dead. You're in my
care. You'll do as I tell you. Now, eat up like a good
little girl."

Briar looked at her uncle. Her long red hair –
which shone like polished copper in the sun – fell like
a curtain across her face, covering one eye. But it
wasn't enough to hide the expression on her face
– pure anger.

"No," she said.

The Pitbull rose from his seat. Slowly, he walked
the length of the table. He stood directly behind his
niece, towering over her.

He reached down, picked up her fork and held it
out to her.

"Take this and eat your breakfast, you ungrateful
little wretch," he hissed. "There will be nothing else."

Briar looked at the fork for a long time. Eventually,
she reached out and took it. The Pitbull leaned
over his niece, placing his hands on either side of

her plate, palm-down on the table. She would learn some manners – by force if necessary.

Briar hovered the fork over one of the eggs. She looked straight ahead, and clenched her teeth.

"EAT! NOW!" he roared.

With the speed of a cat, Briar jabbed the fork into the back of his right hand.

"AAARGGH!" howled The Pitbull. "YOU SAVAGE LITTLE RAT!"

The Pitbull hissed at Briar like a viper.

"YOU WILL LEARN TO BEHAVE!" he roared. "YOU WILL DO WHAT I TELL YOU!"

The Pitbull's men came running at the sound of their master's voice. They had to restrain Briar, who flew at her uncle. The Pitbull hurriedly took a few steps backwards.

"Get her out of my sight!" he ordered. "Lock her in her room. Give her nothing for the rest of the day – no food, no water. Let's see how you like that, you animal!" Spittle flew from The Pitbull's mouth.

Briar kicked, bit and screamed at the men as she was dragged from the room.

When she was gone, and the sounds of her screams could no longer be heard, The Pitbull tried to sit still as one of his men bandaged his injured hand. But he was in too much of a foul mood. He pushed him away angrily.

"Leave me alone!" he commanded.

He grabbed the newspaper and scanned the pages, trying to take his mind off his troublesome neice. Eventually he calmed down. He began reading a story about a rare species of seabird that was returning from the brink of extinction. There was a picture of it – a plump black-feathered bird skimming above the waves. He wondered what it would taste like. The scientist interviewed for the story said it would be a long recovery process for the species.

'You can't hurry nature', he told the journalist.

But lately The Pitbull had been thinking exactly the opposite. His dragon's egg, which had been sitting in a specially constructed room in his private zoo for the past nine months, had shown no signs of hatching. He had spent a fortune on making sure the temperature of the room was just perfect. Another huge sum of money went towards making sure that the entire zoo was fire-proof, just in case the newly hatched dragon tried to burn its way out.

But the egg, which had been obtained at great expense, not to mention huge personal embarrassment, sat as still as a rock in his zoo. Day after day, he stared at it for over an hour, waiting for something to happen. But nothing did. Of course, he had no idea how long a dragon's egg normally takes to hatch. He also had no way of finding out – he certainly couldn't read it in a book.

What if, thought The Pitbull, he was to hit the egg with a hammer and chisel? To open up a small crack, just to help the baby dragon on its way?

The Pitbull rose from his seat. He was decided. He called loudly for his men.

"Get me a hammer and chisels and bring them to the egg room – now!" he barked. "Let's see if we can meet our little dragon – today!" He strode from the room, full of purpose. In the hallway, he pushed the button for the lift. It seemed to take forever, so he jabbed at it several more times. Finally it arrived, and The Pitbull stepped in. He told his men to wait for the next one, then descended the forty floors to ground level alone.

It was a long walk to the zoo through the endless rooms and corridors of The Pitbull's enormous home – giving him more than enough time to begin doubting his plan. What if putting a crack in the egg simply killed the baby dragon inside? Then it would never hatch and he would be back where he started almost a year ago.

The thought made him angry. He cast his mind back over the past year. He remembered when the pilot of his private jet first told him about the dragons. He'd seen some while flying over a remote island, five hundred miles out to sea. The Pitbull couldn't believe it. In fact, he'd refused to believe it. He thought the man had gone mad, and had him sent to the hospital so they could test his mind. But the man was released a week later, pronounced perfectly healthy, yet still telling the same story. The Pitbull sent another pilot and two photographers, in a smaller plane, to find out if it was actually true.

Within a month they had proof: dragons existed. Real, living, fire-breathing, roaring dragons. It was astonishing. Incredible. The stuff of dreams. The Pitbull suddenly saw his destiny – to be known forever as the man who discovered that dragons were real.

He'd thought it would be as easy as taking candy from a baby. The island was deserted apart from one family – a father and mother, with three young children – two boys and a girl. Nothing to worry about… or so he thought.

The Pitbull sent his three best men. He gave them orders to kill a dragon. He planned to stuff its body and display it in his hallway to impress his guests. He also ordered them to bring back a dragon's egg, so that he could hatch it in his private zoo.

Yet, when they arrived back three days later, they'd brought back only the egg. They had somehow been outsmarted by the two boys, who had stopped them from killing a dragon. He didn't bother listening to the men's excuses. In fact, it was only because they had successfully managed to find a dragon's egg that he didn't have them tied to a large concrete block and thrown into the deepest part of the ocean. He ordered the men to be held in his prison for three months as punishment.

The Pitbull's thoughts were interrupted by the ferocious roar of a huge male lion. The giant creature lunged against its cage as he entered the zoo. Row after row of cages lined the sides of the walkway, each occupied by one of the deadliest animals known to exist. A rare snow leopard was in the cage next to the lion, and then came a Bengal tiger. As he continued, he passed a cougar, a black panther, and a cheetah. Each threw itself against the iron bars as he walked by. The Pitbull smiled. His zookeepers were under orders not to feed the animals very much, so they were always angry.

Next came the large amphibians – a saltwater crocodile from Costa Rica, and a Nile crocodile from Egypt. Then came a huge alligator, and a gharial, which is from Nepal, and a black caiman from South America. Each and every one of them could bite off his leg and swallow it whole.

And so it went on – the twenty deadliest snakes in the world, and a section containing the fiercest of the small creatures – a wolverine, Tasmanian devil, and a honey badger. Further on was a large aquarium. Inside swam gigantic great white, tiger, and bull sharks. There was also a blue-ringed octopus, a box jellyfish, puffer and spine fish, and a host of other beautiful but incredibly deadly sea creatures. There wasn't a single animal in The Pitbull's zoo that could not inflict a nasty injury or bring about an early death.

The Pitbull felt right at home.

His men had caught up to him by the time he arrived at a room made completely from bullet-proof glass the colour of smoke. When The Pitbull

tapped a long code into a keypad outside the heavy door, the glass suddenly cleared, revealing what was inside.

As usual, there was no change in the egg. It sat on its stand in the centre of the room, oval and grey. Completely lifeless. It was as if it was a sculpture of an egg, carved from rock by an artist, rather than a real one.

The door slid silently open and The Pitbull walked in.

"Same as ever," he said. "Like a stone."

The Pitbull put one hand out to the side, palm upwards. He was expecting one of his men to rush forward and place the hammer and chisel into it, but instead they just stood watching him, wondering what on earth he was doing.

"You idiots!" he yelled. "The hammer! The chisel! BRING THEM TO ME!"

The man holding the tools rushed forward and gave them to The Pitbull.

"Get out!" he yelled. "Leave me!"

When The Pitbull was left alone, he began circling the egg. He looked carefully at its surface. From a few feet away, it appeared completely grey. On closer inspection, he saw little flecks of white, very like the tiny sparkles of quartz visible in river rocks.

"Where shall I crack it?" The Pitbull asked himself. "Let's start at the top."

Carefully placing the sharp blade of the chisel against the egg, The Pitbull tapped gently with the hammer.

"Easy does it," he said, concentrating fiercely on the task.

After five minutes of tapping, he moved in for a closer look.

"Not even scratched," he said with surprise.

The Pitbull raised the hammer a little higher and brought it down with a little more force.

Nothing.

"Harder," he said to himself.

He tried again, still harder.

Not even the smallest chip flew from the egg.

The Pitbull had run out of patience. Raising the hammer high above his head, he brought it down with all his might.

CLACK!

A violent vibration went through the chisel and up The Pitbull's arm, making his vision blur.

Again, he swung as hard as he could.

CLACK!

Again, the awful vibration. Pain ran up and down his arm. The fork injury on the back of his hand throbbed. Again, no visible damage to the egg.

"Curse you!" he yelled.

THUD!

"AAAAAARRRRRRRGGGGGHHHH!"

The Pitbull rolled on the floor, tears squeezing from his eyes. He clutched his finger. He had completely missed the chisel and hit the index finger on his left hand. His men burst in through the door, alarmed by his cries.

The Pitbull was furious. He yelled at his men to find a crowbar and a sledgehammer. He sent another man running for the first aid kit; his finger was bleeding badly.

While he was being bandaged, The Pitbull had another idea. He sent a third man to find a jackhammer – the kind road workers use for breaking through concrete.

When all was found and brought to the egg room, The Pitbull ordered his men to attack the egg.

First, they used the crowbar. It worked well, taking out small chips each time it struck the egg. But, by now, The Pitbull was tired of waiting.

"GET OUT OF MY WAY!" he yelled, taking up the jackhammer. With a vicious pull of the rip cord, the engine roared to life and the room filled with its smoky exhaust. The Pitbull ran at the egg with all the speed he could muster, holding the jackhammer up in front of him like a lance at a medieval jousting match.

The Pitbull's men leaped out of the way.

The jackhammer struck the egg right in the centre, its steel spike furiously battering at the surface.

There was an almighty crack.

The egg split right down the middle. The two halves fell away from each other, landing with a crash on the concrete floor.

Inside was nothing more than solid rock.

An inhuman scream of rage and frustration burst forth from The Pitbull, so piercing that his men scuttled away in fright.

About the author

Once, when James Russell was a child, he read a book so exciting it made his heart thump in his chest. Now his aim in life is to write books that will do just that for other children. He hopes that this is one of them.

James lives in Auckland, New Zealand with his wife and two young sons, who love adventure in all its forms.

Made in the USA
Monee, IL
03 May 2022